Happy
Birthday
(Yaboinst)
with love
and respect)

Andrew

Nov. 5/1994

Also by Elias Canetti

The Secret Heart of the Clock
Auto-da-Fé
Crowds and Power
Earwitness: Fifty Characters
The Human Province
The Plays of Elias Canetti
The Tongue Set Free: Remembrance of a European Childhood
The Torch in My Ear
The Voices of Marrakesh: A Record of a Visit
The Play of the Eyes
Essays in Honor of Elias Canetti

THE AGONY OF FLIES

ELIAS CANETTI

THE AGONY OF FLIES

Notes and Notations

———

DIE FLIEGENPEIN

Aufzeichnungen

TRANSLATED FROM THE GERMAN BY

H. F. BROCH DE ROTHERMANN

The Noonday Press

Farrar, Straus and Giroux

NEW YORK

Library of Congress catalog card number: 94-71226

*My deep gratitude is expressed to my editor, Sara Bershtel, for her
inspired and thorough suggestions and revisions; she lent wings to
my translation.*
B. de R.

THE AGONY OF FLIES

I

Er wäre zu jeder Zeit gern auf die Welt gekommen, immer wieder, und am liebsten jedesmal für immer.

Sehr vieles weiß man von den Menschen, die man liebt, und hält es doch nicht für wahr.

Das niedrigste Gefühl, das ich kenne, ist der Abscheu vor Unterdrückten, so als hätte man aus ihren Eigenschaften ihre Getretenheit zu rechtfertigen. Von diesem Gefühl sind sehr edle und gerechte Philosophen nicht frei.

Er bemüht sich Menschen mit Großmut anzustecken. Sie werden aber nur größenwahnsinnig.

Viele von uns, zufrieden damit, daß Gott so gut sei, werden selber zu den größten Schurken.

Er stellte alle üblichen Forderungen an sich, aber in einer Fremdsprache.

Es ist schwer, vorsichtige Menschen zu lieben, es sei denn, man sieht, wie ihre Vorsicht alles falsch macht.

Die Vögel tanzen, wenn sie zusammen nach Afrika fliegen. Ihre Rhythmen, feiner und voller als die unseren, entstammen

I

He would have been happy to come into this world at any time, again and again, and if possible, for ever and ever.

We know many things about those we love—things we nevertheless refuse to believe.

There is nothing more base than a certain loathing for the oppressed that goes to great lengths to justify their down-trodden state by pointing to their shortcomings. Not even great and lofty philosophers are entirely free of this failing.

He takes pains to infect others with magnanimity, but they merely break out into megalomania.

Many of us, thoroughly convinced that God is good, are more than content to behave like the worst of scoundrels.

He placed all the usual demands on himself, but in a foreign language.

It is difficult to love cautious people, unless one keeps in mind that their caution distorts everything.

When the birds flock together to fly to Africa, they dance. Their rhythms, fuller and more subtle than our own, are

dem Flügelschlag. Sie stampfen den Boden nicht, aber sie schlagen die Luft, die ist ihnen gut gesinnt. Uns aber haßt die Erde.

Er ist klug wie ein *Rad*.

Keine Schrift ist geheim genug, daß der Mensch sich wahrhaftig in ihr äußerte.

Die Namen der Musikinstrumente sind ein Zauber für sich. Gäbe es nichts anderes, das von uns benannt ist, wir müßten über uns staunen.

Er lobt gern Leute, die es ohnehin zu nichts bringen können. Vorsichtig wird er, wenn jemand Begabung zeigt.

Seine Freunde entzünden und sie dann allein abbrennen lassen, wie grausam und wie natürlich für einen Dichter!

In die indischen Religionen allein ist der Ekel vor der Wiederholung eingegangen, nach unsagbaren Exzessen der Wiederholung, wie sie kein anderes Volk kennt.

Er hoffte, von Gott unbemerkt, lange zu leben.

Die Menschen lieben einen Dichter nur, weil er mit der Zeit verschwenderisch umgeht. Sobald er damit zu sparen beginnt, behandeln sie ihn wie jeden anderen.

born in the beating of their wings. They do not stomp the ground, but gently beat the air, which is well disposed toward them. We, on the other hand, are hated by earth.

He is as ingenious as a *wheel*.

No code is secret enough to allow for the expression of complete candor.

The names of musical instruments have a magic all their own. Had we named nothing else, we still would have reason to marvel at ourselves.

He enjoys praising people who clearly will never amount to anything. But he becomes wary whenever someone shows true talent.

To inflame one's friends and then abandon them to the fire—how cruel, and yet how natural for a poet!

Only the Indian religions exhibit a distaste for repetition, and that only after unspeakable excesses in repetition such as no other people have ever experienced.

His hope was to have a long life, unnoticed by God.

People love a poet merely because he is profligate with his time. As soon as he begins to be stingy with it, they treat him like anyone else.

Du hast Angst vor allem, was nach dem Tod *nicht* kommt.

Ihr zuliebe preßte er sein Herz wie eine Zitrone aus. Aber es gewann sie der andere, der den Zucker dazu sprach.

Er ist so konziliant, daß er vergißt, mit wem er gestern verhandelt hat.

Oft wird ihm der eigene Schatten zu schwer.

Die Löcher des Wissens wandern.

Sie ist zu kurz für ihre Habgier: nirgends langt sie hin.

Der Geizige wird am schwersten unsterblich.

Unter den Toten finden sich auch die Tiere, die nicht gefressen wurden.

Die Tiere in unserem Denken müssen wieder mächtig werden, wie in der Zeit vor ihrer Unterwerfung.

Einfacher sein – du redest so, als ob du gesandt wärest. Leg die Sporen der Überlegenheit ab, steig hinunter vom prahlerischen Roß der nächsten dreitausend Jahre, leb solange du lebst, dränge dich nicht in eine Zeit hinein, in der du ohnehin nicht da bist, laß die Absichten schlafen, vergiß den Namen, vergiß dich, vergiß deinen Tod!

You are afraid of everything that will *not* happen after death.

He squeezed his heart out like a lemon just for her. But the man who won her was the one whose words were the sugar to go with it.

He is so accommodating that he forgets with whom he negotiated the day before.

There are many times when his own shadow is too much for him to bear.

The gaps in our knowledge keep roaming.

She is too short for her own greed: everything is beyond her reach.

The road to immortality is hardest for the miser.

Among the dead may be counted also those animals who were not devoured.

The animals in our thinking must regain the power they held before we subdued them.

Be more simple—you hold forth as if you had been sent from on high. Cast off the spurs of superiority, dismount from the flamboyant steed of the next three thousand years and, instead, live as long as you're alive, don't foist yourself upon a time in which you won't even exist, let all intentions sleep, forget your name, forget yourself, forget your death!

Seine Verzweiflungen sind mir zu pünktlich.

Er ist so schlecht, daß sein Ohr sich vor seiner Zunge fürchtet.

Er kann seine Überzeugungen auseinandernehmen und wieder frisch zusammensetzen.

Es ist sein Traum, die Menschen, die er liebt, auf gesonderten Sternen anzusiedeln.

Manche Menschen sind so niedrig, daß man ihnen nicht die Meinung sagen kann, man findet keine Maske bei ihnen, die sich zum Angesprochenwerden eignet.

Wer zu wenig Menschen kennt, kennt bald nur noch Teufel.

Silben, die vor hunderttausend Jahren gang und gäbe waren.

Er lächelte mit zwanzig Gesichtern, in jedem war er anders, er lächelte freundlich, er lächelte feindlich, er versprach, er hielt hin, er lehnte ab, er verriet, man war es immer zufrieden, denn die verbleibenden Gesichter leuchteten wie unter der Oberfläche des Meeres hervor, und es war schön, sie zu erwarten, bevor sie hinaufgelangt waren.

In Zeiten starken Mißtrauens schafft man aus den Menschen, die man gut kennt oder mit denen man zuletzt gesprochen hat, geheimnisvolle und gefährliche Figuren: sie sagen einem,

As far as I'm concerned, he despairs with excessive punctuality.

He is so evil that his ear is terrified of his tongue.

He is able to dismantle his convictions and then piece them back together.

His dream is to settle the people he loves on separate stars.

There are people so vile you can't even tell them off; they possess not a single mask worth addressing.

Whoever knows too few people, soon will know only devils.

Phrases that were tried and true a hundred thousand years ago.

He smiled with twenty faces and each one revealed a different man—he smiled amiably, he smiled fiendishly, he promised, he delayed, he refused, he betrayed, and yet no one seemed to mind, for the remaining faces shimmered as if from beneath the sea and it was a pleasure to await their rising to the surface.

In times of deep mistrust one tends to transform close friends as well as chance acquaintances into mysterious and dangerous characters: guided by the worst of intentions, they

in der bösesten Absicht, lauter tückische und abträgliche Dinge. Man antwortet ihnen scharf. Sie geben es einem schärfer zurück. Sie haben es nur darauf abgesehen, einen mehr und mehr aufzuregen, bis Zorn und Angst einen zwingen, alle Rücksicht zu vergessen und ihnen ihre schlechtesten Züge, ins Dämonische gesteigert, vors Auge zu halten. Sie erbleichen, vielleicht stellen sie sich sogar für eine Zeit tot. Aber dann plötzlich greifen sie einen wieder an, am liebsten vom Rücken her. Man verbeißt sich in endlose Dialoge mit ihnen. Immer verstehen sie einen, immer versteht man sie, es ist alles in seiner Feindseligkeit gleichmäßig klar. Wahrscheinlich wollen einen diese Figuren fressen, und der Teil der eigenen Person fühlt sich am meisten bedroht, der ihnen zunächst erreichbar ist. Man zieht die Hand rasch zurück, man versteckt seine Leber, man rollt die Zunge ein, obwohl man tüchtig mit ihr weiterredet. Die feindliche Figur ist fest umrissen nur im Haß, den sie für einen äußert und den man ihr wiedergibt. Aber sie kann nicht überall zubeißen, sie hat eine eigentümliche Beschränktheit in ihrer Abhängigkeit von einem selbst. Sie ist wie ein Rauch entstanden und wie einen Rauch bläst man sie hin und her. Sie zittert, sie quillt, kein Wirbeltier, und manchmal denke ich, sie ist eine Erinnerung an die Zeit, da wir am Meeresgrund lebten und von formlosen Geschöpfen angefaßt wurden.

Sobald aber der wirkliche Mensch, dem die Figur ihren Namen verdankt, einem entgegentritt, zergeht sie in nichts, und für den Augenblick ist man froh und beruhigt.

Ein Gott, der die Menschen nicht erschaffen, sondern *gefunden* hat.

Zu viel geistige Erfahrung will ihre Tragezeit; man kann nicht ungestraft lernen, das Gelernte vergißt sich nur langsam, und es ist das Vergessene allein, das die neuen Wege geht.

tell you nothing that is not insidious and mean. You answer them sharply. They retort with even greater venom. Their sole purpose is to upset you more and more until anger and fear compel you to forget all discretion and to confront them with their own worst characteristics, distorted to demonic proportions. They blanch; they even may play dead for a while. But then all of a sudden they return to the attack, preferably from behind. You get locked in endless dialogues with them. They understand you, you understand them, always and without exception: in this mutual animosity everything is crystal-clear. In all probability, these creatures want to eat you alive, and so the part of you that happens to be closest to them feels the most threatened. Quickly you withdraw your hand, hide your liver, roll up your tongue —all the while continuing to move it in furious speech. Your enemy clearly is defined solely by the hatred he bears toward you and that you return in kind. But he cannot strike just anywhere, for he is strangely restricted through his dependency on you. Your enemy appeared just like smoke and, just like smoke, can be blown hither and thither. He trembles, he swells, he is not a vertebrate, and sometimes I'm convinced he is merely a memory of those times when we still lived at the bottom of the ocean and at the mercy of formless creatures.

But as soon as the real individual, whose name the imagined figure bears, steps up and faces you, the figment vanishes into thin air, and for the time being you are cheerful and relieved.

A god who did not create humans but, rather, *found* them.

An excess of spiritual experience takes a longer time to bear fruit; one cannot learn with impunity, what once has been learned is slow to be forgotten, and yet only what has been forgotten is liable to open new paths.

Es wird nie ein Denker aus ihm: er wiederholt sich zu selten.

Das Benennen ist der große und ernste Trost des Menschen.

Und immer erwartet man vom Hauch der Tiere, daß er sich zu neuen unerhörten Worten formt.

Er verkleidet seine Bilder mit Vorwürfen.

Der Sprache bin ich noch immer nicht gram: die triumphierende Bestie der Technik hat ihr etwas von ihrer Würde zurückgegeben.

Der Erfolg ist nur der allerkleinste Teil der Erfahrung.

Sein Gedächtnis haßt ihn, es meldet sich immer dann, wenn er den Mund halten sollte.

Einer läßt alle aufmarschieren, die zu Unrecht vor ihm gestorben sind, und hält ihnen eine Predigt über seine eigene Tüchtigkeit, Sicherheit und Gerissenheit.

Die Krähen über dem gelben Korn geben ihm das heftigste Gefühl des Lebens.

Er ist so stolz, daß er Gott immer etwas schenken möchte.

He will never be a thinker: he doesn't repeat himself enough.

The act of naming is the great and solemn consolation of mankind.

We keep expecting that the breath of animals will turn into new words never heard before.

His images are veiled with reproaches.

I still hold no grudge against language: the triumphant beast of technology has restored some of its dignity.

Success is only the tiniest fraction of experience.

His memory hates him: it always intrudes just when he should hold his tongue.

A certain man summoned everyone who unjustly had died before he did, and proceeded to deliver to them a sermon on his own competence, infallibility, and shrewdness.

The crows above the yellow corn arouse in him the most intense feeling of life.

He is so proud that he's always trying to offer God a gift.

Er hat sich eine tiefe Verehrung für alte Leute bewahrt: er bewundert an ihnen jedes Jahr, das er selbst nicht erlebt hat. Er betet Kinder an: sie verheißen ihm jedes Jahr, das er nicht mehr erleben wird.

Man kann sein Unglück nur verwinden, indem man es spielt.

Die Bedeutung eines Geistes ist zu messen an der Zahl der Jahre, die er verlieren kann.

Immer ist die Zukunft falsch: wir haben *zuviel* Einfluß auf sie.

Er wünscht sich die Existenz der Menschen, die er liebt, aber ohne ihre Gegenwart und ihre Geschäftigkeiten.

Geschöpfe, die in einer Zwischenzeit leben, die neben unserer herläuft, sie durchdringt ohne sie zu berühren, so als ob es Zeitschatten gäbe, die eine eigene Welt für sich ausmachen.

›Gold‹ spricht er aus, als hätte er es gestohlen.

Die Eifersucht wäre abzuteilen, je nachdem was einer am meisten haßt: seine Vor-, seine Neben-, seine Nachbuhler.

Er möchte Augenblicke, die so lange brennen wie ein Zündholz.

He holds old people in the utmost esteem: he admires in them every year he has not yet experienced. He adores children: they evoke in him every year he no longer will experience.

The only way to overcome misfortune is to act it out.

The significance of a great mind may be measured by the number of years it can afford to lose.

The future is always wrong: we exert *too much* influence over it.

He desires the existence of the people he loves, but not their presence and not their preoccupations.

Creatures who inhabit an in-between time which runs parallel to our own, a time that penetrates our own but does not touch it, as if there were such a thing as time-shadows forming a world of their own.

He pronounces the word "gold" as if he had stolen it.

Jealousy should be classified according to whom someone hates the most: past, present, or future rivals.

He wishes for moments that burn as long as a match.

Eine neue Art von Kindern, die in Kriegen nicht da sind.

Der Heilige: er verbringt sein Leben damit zu erklären, was alles er auf keinen Fall täte.

Er ißt die Weisheit mit Stäbchen, auf Chinesisch.

Er denkt in Tieren, wie andere in Begriffen.

Am allerliebsten hat sich der Mensch als blindwütiger Anhänger.

Der Besessene ist nie dankbar.

Die verschwundenen Völker rächen sich.

Bei der Verwirrung zu Babel hat Gott sich verrechnet. Sie sprechen jetzt alle dieselbe Technik.

Von Zeit zu Zeit wäscht er die Fetzen seines Lebens.

Er sagt nie mehr als einen Vokal.

Wer genug gelernt hat, hat nichts gelernt.

A new kind of children who are not around in times of war.

The saint: he spends his life explaining all the things he would never ever do.

He eats wisdom with chopsticks, the Chinese way.

He thinks in animals the way others think in concepts.

Man likes himself best of all as a blindly raging disciple.

He who is obsessed is never grateful.

The vanished nations take their revenge.

God made a mistake in his calculations at the Tower of Babel: nowadays everybody speaks the same technology.

From time to time he washes the tatters of his life.

He never says more than a single vowel.

He who has learned enough has learned nothing.

Er rühmt seine Galeeren, wo die Sklaven auf Polstern sitzen und silberne Ruder führen.

Er ist klug wie eine Zeitung. Er weiß alles. Was er weiß, ist jeden Tag anders.

Er sucht sich glückliche Adjektive, leckt sie ab und klebt sie zusammen.

Er bewertet Frauen nach dem Glück und Männer nach dem Unglück, dessen sie fähig sind.

Das Unglück des Wissens, wenn es sich unverändert weitergibt.

Es sollten die *körperlich* weiterwachsen können, denen es sehr um Größe zu tun ist, bis ins Endlose, und die Menschen hätten vor ihnen Ruhe.

Auch den großen Philosophen macht die Übertreibung, aber sie braucht bei ihm ein sehr dichtgewobenes Kleid von Vernünftigkeit. Der Dichter stellt sie nackt und schimmernd hin.

Sie will ganz genommen werden, mit ihrem vollen Gepäck, und fürchtet, man könnte vor Glück eine Nadel vergessen.

Er sammelt Sündenböcke, um ihre Lasten gerechter zu verteilen.

He boasts about his galleys, where the slaves sit on cushioned seats and row with silver oars.

He is as smart as a newspaper: he knows everything and what he knows changes from day to day.

He looks for happy adjectives, licks them clean, and pastes them together.

He rates women by their capability for happiness, men by their capability for despair.

The calamity of knowledge when it is passed on unchanged.

Those who are very concerned with greatness should be able to grow and grow, *physically,* into infinity. Then they would leave the rest of us in peace.

Even the great philosopher benefits from exaggeration, but with him she must wear a very tightly woven garment of reason. The poet, on the other hand, exposes her in all her shimmering nudity.

She wants someone to take her whole, with all her baggage; but she fears that, in his joy, he might forget a needle.

He collects scapegoats so as to redistribute their burdens more fairly.

Er mischt in jeden Satz zumindest ein fremdes Wort, aus einer Sprache die er nicht kennt, auch die Anwesenden nicht, und alle nicken einander vertraulich zu.

Es gibt für nichts wirklich Ersatz, das roheste Ziel meldet sich wieder, die Triebe sind zwar elastisch, aber unbarmherzig, und ihr Gedächtnis für die gezählten Gegenstände, auf die es ihnen ankommt, ist unzerstörbar.

Er *spart* sich seinen Ruhm zusammen.

Man braucht einen sehr großen Schatz an fremden Namen, nach deren Sinn man nicht einmal fragen möchte.

Der Haß hat ein eigenes Klopfen des Herzens.

Der Gestaltlose kann sich nicht verwandeln.

Immer wenn er ein *falscher* Prophet sein will, trifft alles ein.

Er ist unglücklich, wenn er einen Tag nichts zu *zählen* hatte.

Es ist leicht, vernünftig zu sein, wenn man niemand, auch sich selber nicht, liebt.

Er würde sich, wenn es nach ihm ginge, von einigen wenigen Göttern beschenken lassen, die er aber nicht darum bittet, und dann mit ihren Geschenken dasselbe tun wie sie.

Each of his sentences contains at least one word from a language neither he nor anyone else present knows, at which all nod to one another in smug satisfaction.

There are no real substitutes for anything, even the crudest goals continue to draw us on, and even though our instincts are quite flexible, they are also merciless and their memory for the few objects that really matter to them is indestructible.

He *scrapes* together his fame, bit by bit.

Needed: a large treasure trove of foreign names, the meanings of which one doesn't care to inquire about.

Hatred has its own peculiar heartbeat.

That which has no form cannot transform itself.

Every time he aspires to be a *false* prophet, everything he says comes true.

He is unhappy if a single day goes by with nothing to *count*.

 It's easy to be reasonable when you don't love anyone, including yourself.

If he could have his way, he would receive presents from just a few of the gods—though without ever asking. He would accept their presents and then dispose of them just as they do.

Die intime Art eines Menschen, die ihn entzückt – wie er sie haßt, wenn sie für jeden, wenn sie für alle dieselbe ist! Wie ihm dann jede schnöde, jede abscheuliche Kälte lieber wäre! Er lebt in der Vorstellung, daß zu jedem Menschen nur eine ganz bestimmte Verhaltensweise möglich ist, und wer sie nicht hat, der *verwechselt* die Leute.

An schönen Tagen fühlt er sich seines Lebens zu sicher.

Befreundete Heiden legten ihn in seinem Paradies ab und nahmen sofort Reißaus.

Die feurigen Räder der Sterne bei Anaximander und ihre Raserei bei Van Gogh.

Er befaßt sich mit der Geschichte, um sie der Menschheit abzunehmen.

Gott liebt es nicht, daß man Lehren aus der neueren Geschichte zieht.

Seit den Hexen nichts mehr geschieht, sind sie harmlos.

Das Größte an der Liebe ist, daß in ihr alle Rechte aufgehoben sind.

Das vollkommenste und furchterregendste Kunstwerk der Menschheit ist ihre Einteilung der Zeit.

The intimate ways and gestures of someone he finds enchanting—how he loathes it if they are bestowed upon everyone alike! How much he then would prefer the rankest, the most repellent coldness! He harbors the illusion that for every individual there is one and only one pattern of behavior, and that he who does not demonstrate this is simply *mistaking* one person for another.

On fair days he feels too sure of his own life.

Friendly heathens delivered him to his paradise and immediately took to their heels.

The fiery wheels of Anaximander's stars and their frenzy in Van Gogh.

He deals with history so that mankind won't have to do so.

God does not like us to draw lessons from recent history.

Witches became harmless the moment they no longer were subject to persecution.

The greatest thing about love is that within its domain all rights are abolished.

Man's most perfect and awe-inspiring work of art is his organization of time.

Tatsachen lassen sich *nicht* zusammensetzen. Es ist am besten, man bekommt sie, sobald sie abgekocht und erstarrt sind, einzeln vorgeworfen. Auf diesem Prinzip beruht die Wirkung Suetons.

Es ist die Gelehrsamkeit nur derer erträglich, die dem Tod keine Ehren erweisen.

Die Leute reden, als hätten sie immer schon so geredet.

Sie kauft sich ein billiges Rückgrat.

Einer, der die Menschen haßt, weil sie sich willig unter die Herrschaft von Explosionen gebeugt haben.

Man kann Geschichte so schreiben, als hätte es immer wie zu unserer Zeit ausgesehen. Aber wozu schreibt man dann Geschichte?

Sein Denken hat Flossen statt Flügel.

Die gierigsten Fische schmecken ihr am besten.

Sobald es einmal geschehen ist, läuft in der Geschichte alles am Schnürchen.

Facts *cannot* be pieced together. It is best to get them after they've been boiled hard and solid, then tossed to us one by one. This principle accounts for the lasting effect of the works of Suetonius.

Only the erudition of those who show no respect for death is bearable.

People speak as if they'd always spoken that way.

She buys herself a bargain backbone.

A man who hates mankind because it willingly submitted to the tyranny of explosions.

One can write history as if it had always looked the way it does today. But then why write history at all?

His thoughts have fins instead of wings.

She finds that the greedier the fish, the better the taste.

Once it happened, everything in history runs as smooth as clockwork.

Der Selbstmord wird den Menschen bewahrt bleiben, aber er muß zu einem unheimlichen und seltenen Ereignis werden, ein einziger Selbstmord wie früher ein Krieg.

Scylla und Charybdis des Geistes: zu Vieles sagen oder Weniges zu oft.

Schlechter als das eigene macht ihn das Elend der anderen.

Die Philosophen nicht danach beurteilen, ob sie gerade jetzt recht haben.

Wie vieles weiß man, bloß weil es einen nichts angeht!

Schon um der Farben willen ließe es sich ewig leben.

Die Geschichte enthält *jeden* Sinn und ist darum sinnlos.

Wer denken will, muß es aufgeben, zu *werben*.

Die Zeit, die er verschenkt, ist zu kostbar, um verkauft zu werden.

Gott versprach sich, als er den Menschen schuf.

Was wären Augen ohne ihre Besonnenheit, ohne die Lider?

Suicide will stay with us, but it must become an odd and rare occurrence—every single suicide as singular as a war in ages past.

The Scylla and Charybdis of the mind: to say either too much or too little too often.

Other people's misery makes him feel worse than his own.

Philosophers should not be judged by whether they happen to be right just now.

How much we know only because it's none of our business!

For the sake of the colors alone it would be worthwhile to live forever.

History contains *every* meaning and is therefore meaningless.

Whoever wishes to think has to give up *promoting* his own thoughts.

The time he gives away is far too precious to be sold.

God must have misspoken when He created Man.

What would eyes be without their caution—without lids?

Utopien haben etwas *Bescheidenes*, das die Menschen von ihnen abstößt.

Die heidnischen Stimmen der Vögel.

Eine erstarrte Gruppe von Menschen, jeder die Krallen im Fleisch des anderen, lachende Gesichter, lüstern und von Schmerz verzerrt.

Die trostlosen Einleitungen zu Meisterwerken, abschrekkend, dürr, erhaben oder unverschämt! O warum ist man neugierig! Warum muß ein Dichter geboren sein und warum gestorben! Genügt es nicht, daß er einen Namen trägt, und ist ihm nicht dieser schon schwer genug? Aber die Leute kennen kein Erbarmen. Sie müssen ihren Dichter kochen, würzen und essen.

Vor allem bemüht er sich, den Leuten seine eigenen schlechten Eigenschaften abzugewöhnen.

Das Denken wird klarer, sobald man sich mit den Formen der Tiere vertraut gemacht hat.

Die verschiedenen Künste sollen miteinander in keuschester Beziehung leben.

Liebe, frei von Todesangst um das geliebte Wesen? – und wenn es das gäbe, wäre es wert, Liebe zu heißen?

Utopias possess a kind of *modesty* which repels people.

The heathen voices of birds.

A group of people, each frozen with his claws embedded in the flesh of another, laughing faces, bursting with lust and distorted in pain.

The disheartening introductions to masterworks, desolate, arid, sublime, or impudent! Oh, why are people curious? Why must a poet be born and why must he die? Is it not enough that he must bear a name—isn't that a sufficiently heavy burden by itself? But people have no mercy. They insist on cooking their poet, seasoning him, and then devouring him.

He mostly keeps himself busy breaking other people of his own bad habits.

Thinking becomes clearer as soon as one has learned the shapes of animals.

The separate arts should live in the most chaste cohabitation.

A love free of all mortal fear for one's beloved? Even if such a thing existed, would it deserve to be called love?

Sie ißt aus Zorn, sie ißt aus Enttäuschung, sie ißt aus Liebe, sie ißt aus Gram. Aus Bescheidenheit, Stolz und Sehnsucht ißt sie. Sie hat sich aus dem Leib ihrer Mutter hinausgegessen. Im Grab, wenn sie nichts anderes hat, wird sie Sarg und Nägel essen.

Er hat einen Sack voll Namen, in vielen Sprachen, die Dinge selber hat er draußen liegen lassen.

Die Kindheit wird voller, je älter man wird, und es ist nicht gleichgültig, wenn man seinen ersten Jahren das Maß nimmt.

Er will durch die Geschichte seiner Kindheit Europa vereinigen.

(1943)

Die Ströme der Dichtung fließen überall und sie müssen nicht ineinander münden.

Für den systematischen Geist gibt es nur eine Rettung: die spontane und zufällige Äußerung, die man nicht weiter verfolgt. Sie darf sich nur nicht für ein Gesetz oder eine Großmacht ausgeben.

Der Tod schweigt über nichts.

Der Geist soll sich bisweilen im Erzählen einer sehr langen Geschichte sammeln. Von Nadeln und Grausamkeit allein kann er nicht leben. Er braucht auch zärtliche Fäden.

She eats out of rage, she eats out of disappointment, she eats out of love, she eats out of sorrow. She eats out of modesty, pride, and longing. She ate herself out of the womb of her mother. And once in the grave, lacking anything else, she'll eat her coffin and its nails.

He has a bag stuffed with names, in many languages, but he left the things themselves lying outside on the ground.

Childhood becomes richer the older one gets and it is no idle task to take the measure of one's first years.

He wants to unify Europe through the story of his childhood.

(1943)

The rivers of poetry flow everywhere, and they do not necessarily converge.

The only salvation for the systematic mind is the spontaneous random remark which is not to be further pursued but which also must not declare itself as the Law.

Death tells all.

When telling a very long story, the mind should collect itself from time to time. It cannot live off needles and cruelty alone. It also requires some tender threads.

Der Mythus ist eine Geschichte, deren Frische mit der Wiederholung zunimmt.

Der Maler und seine Politik: er glaubt, es genügt, die Erde mit anderen Farben zu bemalen.

Der Mensch heute müßte sich um alle inzwischen beschriebenen Tiere besser kennen als die Antike.

Den Mann um Vierzig packt eine verzweifelte Lust, Gesetze zu geben.

Es geschieht immer, was er will, aber nach vier oder fünf Jahren, wenn er längst etwas anderes will.

Ein Künstler, der am größten Tag seines Lebens, mitten unter den Menschen, die ihn feiern, seinen Namen vergißt.

Der Dichter lebt von Übertreibung und durch Mißverständnisse macht er sich bekannt.

In den meisten Religionen heuchelt der Mensch Erniedrigung und springt dann hinterrücks wütend in die Höhe.

Seit die Erde eine Kugel geworden ist, nimmt sie jeder Lump ganz in die Hand.

A myth is a tale that becomes fresher with every retelling.

The painter and his politics: he believes that it's enough to paint the earth with different colors.

Man's self-knowledge should have increased since ancient times by the number of animals described in the interim.

About the age of forty, men suddenly are gripped by the desperate urge to issue laws.

Everything he wants always comes to pass, but only after four or five years, by which time he's long wanted something else.

An artist who, on the most important day of his life and in the midst of people singing his praises, forgets his name.

The poet lives by exaggeration and makes himself known through misunderstandings.

In most religions people fall to their knees in feigned humility, only to leap back up in perfidious rage.

Ever since the earth became a ball, any scoundrel can cup it whole in his hand.

Wie überzeugend klingt alles, wenn man wenig weiß!

Die toten Menschen sind schon zu mächtig in ihm. Was soll aus ihm werden, wenn die toten Tiere über ihn kommen?

Verzweiflung der Helden über die Abschaffung des Todes.

216 000 Worte *am Tag*.

Wieviel Bekehrungen er nur studiert, um selber keiner zu erliegen!

Die Wiedergeburten sind ihm zu ordentlich, er will *zugleich* in vielen verschiedenen Geschöpfen leben.

Ein Bild, irgendein Bild kann die Liebe zu einem Menschen, den man immer um sich hat, bis zum Wahnwitz steigern.

How convincing everything sounds to someone who knows little!

The dead people already wield too much power in him. What shall happen to him when the dead animals overcome him as well?

The despair of the heroes at the abolition of death.

216,000 words *every day*.

The number of conversions he studies in order not to succumb to a single one!

Reincarnations are too methodical for his taste; he aspires to live in any number of different creatures simultaneously.

A single image, any image at all, can heighten to sheer lunacy the love we hold for our constant companions.

II

Er ist so klug, er sieht überhaupt nur, was hinter seinem Rükken geschieht.

Wer Selbsterkenntnisse hinterläßt, wird beim Wort genommen. Welche Tollkühnheit, angesichts der Herzlosigkeit künftiger Geschlechter!

Von allen Hindernissen sind Ströme die lockendsten.

Alle Tatsachen meines eigenen Lebens, ob gut oder schlecht, haben für mich etwas *Störendes*.

Die Handlungen der Menschen gehen mir so nahe wie anderen Wohlgeschmack oder Giftigkeit ihrer Speise.

Seine Verzeichnisse sind seine Versäumnisse.

Viele Philosophen sind des Dichters Tod.

Es ist beschämend, wie man sich gewisse Verwandlungen auf keinen Fall erlauben mag. Der Charakter ist die *Auswahl* unter den Verwandlungen.

II

He is so smart he only sees what's happening behind his back.

Whoever leaves a legacy of self-revelation shall be taken at his word. What a reckless venture, given the fact that future generations will show no pity!

Of all obstacles none is more tempting than rivers.

All the facts of my own life, whether good or bad, are in some way disturbing to me.

The way other people act affects me as much as some people are affected by the pleasant or odious taste of their food.

His lists are composed of nothing but omissions.

A pack of philosophers spells death for the poet.

It is humiliating how we cannot allow ourselves certain changes of character under any circumstances. In fact, character really consists of our *choice* among those changes that are permitted to us.

Die Lust, neue Figuren zu spielen, vor Leuten, die einen sehr
gut kennen, unter der Hand sozusagen ihnen zu entwischen,
ist so groß, daß das Niederschreiben neuer Charaktere, wie es
zum Metier des Dramatikers oder Romanciers gehört, daran
gemessen langweilig wird. Gewiß sind viele der besten Figuren bloß darum nie an die Nachwelt gelangt. Man will sie sein,
intensiv, und mit sichtbar unmittelbarer Zauberwirkung auf
die anderen, nicht bloß sie verzeichnen und bewahren. Es ist
befreiend, wenn diese alten Hände mit neuen Sprachen sprechen, die man noch vor kurzem selbst nicht kannte. Es ist be-
glückend, in ein neues Gesicht zu fahren und das alte wie eine
Maske wieder daran zu hängen.

Die Urenkelin des großen Astronomen hat mich empfangen.
Sie lebt unter den Fernrohren, die die Sterne des nördlichen
wie des südlichen Himmels aufgenommen haben. Ich war im
alten Haus und im Arbeitszimmer Wilhelm Herschels. Genau
gegenüber ein modernes Kinogebäude, vor dem in langer
Reihe Besucher anstehen. Leicht könnten sie die Apparate
und Papiere auf dem Tische Herschels sehen, wissen aber
nicht, daß er gelebt hat. Die Urenkelin wünscht sich, daß jenes Kinogebäude in den Erdboden versenkt würde.

Die Dichter, deren Stätten man besucht, lachen sich eins in
ihre Werke.

Es erregen ihn nur Verdächte und nicht Tatsachen. Diese können noch so arg sein, sie können ärger sein als der Verdacht
selbst – sie machen ihm keine Angst. Sobald eine Tatsache einen Verdacht bekräftigt, wird er ruhig. Er kann zum Beispiel
sehr fürchten, daß man ihn vergiftet hat, aber es gibt ein Mittel
für ihn, seine Furcht loszuwerden: er muß sich nur davon
überzeugen, daß er wirklich vergiftet *ist*, und schon ist alles in
bester Ordnung.

The pleasure of playing new roles in the presence of an audience who knows you very well, to slip, so to speak, surreptitiously out of its grasp—that pleasure is so great that the writing of new characters, as practiced by writers and playwrights, by comparison seems quite boring. This undoubtedly is the reason why some of the best such imagined characters never reach posterity. You wish to *be* these characters with such intensity as to have an immediate effect on others, magically and visibly—instead of merely recording and preserving them on paper. It is liberating when your old hands speak in new languages which a short while ago you had never heard of. And it is blissful to enter a new face and to slip the old one over it like a mask.

The great-granddaughter of the famous astronomer has received me. She lives among the telescopes that have recorded the stars of both the northern and southern skies. I visited the old house and the study that belonged to Wilhelm Herschel. Directly across stands a modern cinema, in front of which people wait in long lines. It would be easy for them to go see the scientific instruments and papers lying on Herschel's desk, but they have no idea that such a man existed. His great-granddaughter would like the movie house to be swallowed by the earth.

When people visit places associated with famous poets, the poets just laugh up the sleeve of their collected works.

Only suspicions upset him, never the actual facts. These facts may be the worst imaginable, even worse than the suspicions—but even so, they inspire no fear in him. As soon as a fact corroborates a suspicion, he regains his composure. For instance, he may be mortally afraid of having been poisoned, but there is one way of overcoming this dread: he merely has to convince himself that he has in truth been poisoned—then everything is fine once more.

Er durchschaut Menschen sehr rasch und verfällt ihnen dann erst recht, weil er sie durchschaut hat.

Es ist eine beinahe unwiderstehliche Versuchung, Kummer zu bereiten, wenn man die Macht hat, ihn wieder aus der Welt zu schaffen.

Das Lesen will sich bei mir durch Lesen fortpflanzen, Anregungen von außen gehorche ich nie, oder nur nach sehr langer Zeit. Ich will *entdecken*, was ich lese. Wer mir ein Buch empfiehlt, schlägt es mir aus der Hand, wer es preist, verleidet es mir auf Jahre. Ich traue nur den Geistern, die ich wirklich verehre. *Sie* können mir alles empfehlen, um meine Neugier zu wecken, genügt es, daß sie etwas in einem Buche *nennen*. Was aber andere nennen, mit ihren flüchtigen Zungen, ist wie mit einem wirksamen Fluch belegt. So hatte ich es schwer, die großen Bücher kennenzulernen, denn das eigentlich Größte ist in den Kult der Allgemeinheit eingegangen. Die Leute haben es auf den Lippen, wie die Namen ihrer Helden, und indem sie es mit vollem Munde sprechen – sie wollen daran recht satt sein –, verwünschen sie mir, was zu kennen für mich so wichtig wäre.

In einzelnen Sätzen ahmt man am wenigsten nach. Schon zwei Sätze beisammen sind wie von jemand anderem.

Ein Land, in dem man nur vor Sehnsucht atmet.

Die Schätzung der Leute richtet sich in England danach, wie sehr sie es verstehen, den anderen in Ruhe zu lassen.

He is very quick to see through people and then he is all the more prone to become their prey precisely because he has seen through them.

The temptation to create grief is virtually impossible to resist—as long as it remains in one's power to remove it once again.

Reading seeks to propagate itself in me by reading; I never follow any outside recommendations, or if I do, then only after a very long time. I want to *discover* what I read. Whoever suggests a book to me knocks it out of my hands; whoever praises it spoils it for me for years. I only trust the minds I truly revere. *They* can recommend anything to me, and to awaken my curiosity all they have to do is to *mention* something in a given book. But whatever others recommend with their facile tongues is as if truly cursed. Thus it was hard for me to get to know the great books, for the greatest works long ago have entered the idolatry of the commonplace. People have the names of those books—as well as their heroes—on the tips of their tongues, and since they are so intent on stuffing themselves, they pronounce these names with their mouths full, thereby spoiling my own appetite for what would be so important for me to know.

Single sentences show imitation least: even two sentences taken together seem as if they had been borrowed from someone else.

A country in which one breathes only out of longing.

In England people are valued according to the extent to which they manage to leave others alone.

Die Kunst ist, wenig genug zu lesen.

Das Häßlichste: ein geiziger Pfau.

Die Bedeutenden sind oft nur die Neugierigen, die sich weit weg gelesen haben.

Er will zerstreute Aufzeichnungen hinterlassen als Korrektur zum geschlossenen System seiner Ansprüche.

Die Geschichte setzt den Mächtigen Hörner auf.

Er will, daß jeder Satz aus dessen eigener Erfahrung spricht.

Die Menschen, die man zu lange kennt, erdrosseln die Figuren, die man gern erfinden möchte.

Die Leute scheuen den, der immer dasselbe sagt. Wenn er es aber rücksichtslos genug sagt, lassen sie sich von ihm beherrschen.

Wieviel Jahrhunderte noch werden bei Plato plündern gehen!

Die Seele ist vielfach, aber sie stellt sich gern, als ob sie einfach wäre.

The trick is to read just little enough.

The epitome of ugliness: a stingy peacock.

The great are often simply those who were curious enough to read themselves into a great remoteness.

He intends to leave behind random notes as a revision of the closed system of his claims.

History makes cuckolds out of the mighty.

He wants every sentence to speak out of its own experience.

The people you know for too long strangle the characters you would like to invent.

People shun the man who always repeats himself. But if he repeats himself with sufficiently inconsiderate relentlessness, they will succumb to his domination.

How many more centuries will go on plundering Plato?

The soul is manifold but likes to give the impression of being simple.

Was sie alles möchte, Abenteuer, Maskenfeste, Gelage und ihn als Zahnstocher dazu.

Sie will nichts von Güte wissen, und er ist wütend darüber.

Wenn die Angst um einen Menschen unerträglich geworden ist, bleibt ihm nur noch ein Mittel, sich davon zu befreien. Er erzählt einem Dritten, der beiden gut bekannt ist, daß jener umgekommen ist. Er beschreibt die Nachricht, den Weg, den sie genommen hat, alle Einzelheiten jenes befürchteten Todes. Er spricht davon mit viel Aufwand und mit genau den Zügen, die ihr gebühren würden, wenn sie wahr wäre. Das Entsetzen, das er so beim Dritten hervorruft, tut ihm unendlich wohl. Nach einer kleinen Weile spricht er mit ihm über ganz andere Dinge, und wenn er ihn verläßt, hat er das sichere Gefühl, daß der Mensch, um den er so sehr gefürchtet hat, lebt und gar nicht in Gefahr ist.

Er ist so ernst, er könnte sich mit einem Regenwurm zerstreiten.

An jener Nachricht über die Mauersegler, die bei Nacht in großen Höhen schlafend fliegen, hat mich ergriffen, daß Traum und Flug noch zusammenfallen.

Er will, daß die Nachrichten an ihn herankommen wie lebende Boten, und er haßt es, sie zu provozieren.

It's amazing all the things she wants: adventures, masked balls, banquets, and what's more—him to serve as her toothpick.

She doesn't want to hear about kindness, and this angers him no end.

When his anxiety about a person becomes unbearable, he is left with only one means to rid himself of it: He tells a third party, well known to both of them, that the person in question has died. He describes the nature of the news and the way it reached him, as well as all the details of that death he so greatly feared. He expounds on it with much emotion and all the facial expressions appropriate to the event, as if it were true. The horrified shock he thus elicits in the third party soothes him tremendously. A little later he talks with him about something else entirely, and upon leaving him, he is filled with the absolute certainty that the person for whose life he had felt such great fear is alive and safe from all danger.

He's so grimly serious he could pick a fight with an earthworm.

I was very moved by that report on chimney swifts, who sleep while flying through the night at great heights, particularly by the fact that dreaming and flying are indivisible.

He wants the news reports to approach him like living messengers, and he hates to provoke them.

Ein Riese, der auf Zehenspitzen »Fliegen von der Decke fängt«. Militär-Pferde im Stall scheuen vor dem Riesen. »Pferde-Augen sollen Gegenstände viel mehr vergrößern als die von Menschen.«

Ein Sterbender, der von seinen Göttern Abschied nimmt.

Jahre meines Lebens gäbe ich dafür, für kurze Zeit ein Tier zu sein.

Alle Literatur schwankt zwischen Natur und Paradies und liebt es, das eine für das andere zu halten.

Mit seinem Wissen schützt sich der Mensch vor der Ewigkeit und bildet sich ein, sie zu erlangen.

Sie streitet, weil sie dann besser weint. Er streitet, weil er dann besser strotzt.

Kämpfe langweilen ihn, weil sie von jeder Erkenntnis abführen.

Niemand erklären, wie verlassen man ist, auch sich selber nicht.

Man hält so lange an sich fest, bis man keine Himmelsrichtung mehr kennt.

A giant who merely has to stand on his tiptoes to "pick flies from the ceiling." In the stables the cavalry horses shy away from the giant. "The eyes of horses supposedly magnify objects much more than human eyes."

A dying man taking leave from his gods.

I happily would trade several years of my life for a short while as an animal.

All literature wavers between nature and paradise and loves to mistake one for the other.

Man uses his knowledge to protect himself from eternity and in so doing imagines he is attaining it.

She fights because thereafter she is better able to weep. He fights because thereafter he is all the more strongly aroused.

Struggles bore him because they lead away from any understanding.

Never tell anyone how forsaken you feel, not even yourself.

A person keeps a hold on himself until he loses all sense of direction.

Er bemüht sich, immer weniger zu wissen und muß dazu eine Menge lernen.

Im Herbst ist die Sonne sich selber dankbar.

Wie gering die Menschen sich ihren Gott denken! *Einen* Traum billigen sie ihm zu, *eine* Schöpfung!
Man könnte aber auch sagen, daß Gott der ist, der alles *auf einmal* träumt.

Am merkwürdigsten sind mir die Dichter, deren knappes Leben von dem ihrer älteren Zeitgenossen noch überholt wird. So kann Kleist in der reiferen Zeit Goethes jung sein, und dann überlebt ihn dieser noch um beinahe zwanzig Jahre. Ausgeprägter ist dieses selbe Verhältnis zwischen Novalis und Goethe, dabei wäre zu bedenken, wieviel Goethe Novalis bedeutet hat. Die jungen Dichter werden leichter zeitlos, ihre Unsterblichkeit ist wie eine Entschädigung: alt sind sie gar nicht zu denken. Man neigt dann dazu zu glauben, sie seien jung gestorben, eben um kein Bild des Alten von sich zu hinterlassen.

Einer der noch im Sterben Vokabeln lernt.

Der Gesinnungslose, der anderen ihre Gesinnung so vorwirft, als ob er selber eine hätte, und je nach den Vorwürfen, die er gerade braucht, immer eine andere.

Er gab sich alle erdenkliche Mühe, aus seinem Feinde Geld herauszukriegen. Dann schickte er es ihm in kleine Fetzen

He takes pains to know less and less and to that end has to learn more and more.

The autumnal sun is grateful to itself.

How puny an image people have formed of their God! All they're willing to grant Him is *one* dream, *one* creation! But it could also be said that God is He who dreams *everything all at once*.

For me, the most remarkable poets are those whose brief life span was exceeded by much older contemporaries. Thus Kleist was still quite young during the mature years of Goethe, who then outlived Kleist by more than twenty years.
This disproportion is even more extreme between Novalis and Goethe, especially when considering how much Goethe meant to Novalis. It is easier for those young poets to become timeless, their immortality seems like a form of compensation: it's impossible to imagine them in old age. We are inclined to believe that they died young in order not to leave behind a single image of their aged selves.

A person who still learns new words even as he's dying.

The man who lacks all conviction and who nevertheless denounces others for theirs, all the while claiming one of his own—which he constantly varies to fit his denunciations of the moment.

He made every effort to extract money from his enemy. Then he sent it back, the bills torn to shreds. That's how

zerrissen zurück. So sehr verachtete er ihn, so sehr verachtete er Geiz, und so sehr wollte er diesen Feind eben in seinem Geize treffen.

Auch die Unsterblichkeit hat ihre Wucherer.

Schwindlerin, die mit letzten Worten hausiert.

Die Mumie des lustigsten Mannes aus dem alten Ägypten.

Die Völker, die sich während der letzten drei- oder viertausend Jahre einen Namen gemacht haben und ihn nun bis zum Ende behalten werden.

Er ist von allem beeindruckt, was er verbessern darf.

Er liebt die Felsen, das Wissen, wegen der ungeheuren Abgründe dazwischen.

Der Blick jahraus jahrein in dieselbe Landschaft wird zu einer besänftigenden Leere, die man nicht erkennt und darum nicht fürchtet.

Er will nicht mehr leben, es sei denn früher.

Die Pflanzen hielt er für beschränkt, die Tiere für überholt.

much he despised him, how much he despised avarice, and how much he wanted to strike this enemy straight in his avaricious heart.

Immortality, too, has its usurers.

A female swindler peddling people's last words.

The mummy of the merriest man of ancient Egypt.

The nations who made a name for themselves in the last three or four thousand years and now shall keep it forever.

He is impressed by anything he is allowed to improve.

He loves both rocky promontories and knowledge because of the abysses gaping between the summits of both.

The view of the same landscape year in and year out becomes a soothing emptiness which one ceases to perceive and therefore ceases to fear.

He no longer has any desire for life—unless it be an earlier one.

He considered plants limited and animals obsolete.

Er stöbert gern in Meinungen herum.

Die Historiker daraufhin untersuchen, was als frühester Glanz in ihr Leben schien.

Eine Versammlung der lebenden englischen Lyriker, in der jeder an Bescheidenheit die erste Stelle einnimmt.

Er kommt sich tiefsinnig vor, denn er ahmt nur die Autoren nach, von denen nicht mehr als abgerissene Sätze übrig sind.

Das Denken verliert seine Wucht, wenn es zum Alltag wird, es soll wie von fernher auf seine Gegenstände stürzen.

Wenn er lange nichts von Göttern gelesen hat, wird er unruhig.

Alle, die er je gekannt hat, bitten ihn ums Wort.

Es ist nur möglich zu leben, weil es so viel zu wissen gibt. Eine gute Weile, nachdem es sich über einen ergossen hat, behält das Wissen noch seine Glätte und Neutralität, wie Öl auf den stürmischen Wassern der Gefühle. Sobald es sich aber mit diesen doch vermischt hat, hilft es einem gar nichts mehr, und man muß neues Wissen auf die Wellen schütten.

Jede geistige Tendenz in seinem Leben wartet ihre Zeit ab, bis sie, zu einer Person gesammelt, ihm entgegentritt und zum Schicksal wird.

He likes to browse in opinions.

A research project focused on historians—to uncover the earliest brightness that shone into their lives.

A gathering of contemporary English poets, each of whom takes first place in modesty.

He deems himself profound, for he imitates only those authors who left behind nothing but a few disjointed fragments.

Thought loses its force (*or* weight) when it becomes commonplace; it should hurl itself upon its subjects as from a great height.

He becomes restless whenever he goes for any length of time without reading about gods.

All those he has ever known ask him to be heard.

It is possible to live only because there is so much to know. For a good while after it has flooded our minds, knowledge still preserves its smoothness and neutrality, like oil poured on the stormy seas of the emotions. But as soon as knowledge has mixed with emotions, it is no longer of any use and new knowledge must then be cast over the waves.

Every spiritual trend in his life bides its time until, assembled into a person, it confronts him and becomes his fate.

Dichter ist, wer Figuren erfindet, die ihm niemand glaubt und die doch keiner vergißt.

Einer, den keiner je wiedersieht. Wie macht er das?

Sie kann nichts aufgeben: wenn einer ihr die Hand gibt, kriegt er nichts mehr zurück.

Eine Welt, in der jeder sterben darf, so oft er Lust hat, aber immer nur für eine beschränkte Zeit.

Ein Mensch, in dem jeder einen anderen Bekannten erkennt.

Er sucht sich einen tauben Gott aus, da kann er beten, was ihm paßt.

In einem sehr verlängerten Leben wird man sich mehr Zeit nehmen können; wenn nur die Mittel zu dieser Verlängerung von den traditionellen Minuten und Sekunden nicht zu sehr verseucht sind. Vielleicht wird man eine neue Zeiteinteilung versuchen müssen.

»Ready to be anything, in the ecstasy of being ever.«
                                                    Sir Thomas Browne

Der Balg der Zeit liegt ausgeweidet am Boden. Nun wollen sie ihn gerben.

A poet is someone who invents characters in whom no one believes yet no one can forget.

Someone whom no one ever sees twice. How does he manage that?

She is incapable of giving up anything: if you offer her your hand, you'll never get it back.

A world in which people are allowed to die as often as they like, but each time only for a limited period.

Someone in whom each person recognizes a different acquaintance.

He chooses a god who is deaf, so that he may pray any way he likes.

In a greatly extended life people will be able to take more time for everything, as long as the means for such extension are not too heavily infected by the traditional minutes and seconds. It may be that we'll have to try some new arrangement of time.

"Ready to be anything, in the ecstasy of being ever."
                                        Sir Thomas Browne

The hide of time lies disemboweled on the ground. Now they want to tan it.

Die Geschichte weiß alles besser, weil sie nichts weiß.

Ich möchte nicht sterben, ohne jeden Glauben wenigstens geträumt zu haben.

In der Nähe der gefährlichen Grenzen sieht er sich um. Er hat viel übersehen, aber es ist noch dort. Sein Auge reicht weit zurück, es ist wie ein klingender Himmel und legt sich zärtlich über das Versäumte.

Wenn der Mensch sehr glücklich ist, erträgt er keine fremde Musik.

Die Meinungen haben ihre Nachbarschaften, manche sind sich über eine ganz enge Gasse hinüber feind.

Gogols letzte Worte: »Eine Leiter, rasch, eine Leiter!«

»Alles ist schon dagewesen, nur ich nicht«, der höhnische Kernsatz der Macht.

Gott klaubt rasch ein paar Sterne zusammen, um sie vor uns zu retten.

Der Regen macht mich glücklich, als wäre ich eben leicht und schmerzlos auf die Welt gekommen.

History knows everything better because it knows nothing at all.

I don't want to die without at least having dreamt every faith.

Close to the dangerous borders he looks around. He has overlooked a great deal, but it is all still there. His eye reaches far back, it is like a ringing sky, tenderly covering all that was missed.

When people are very happy, they cannot bear any music that is foreign to them.

Opinions have their own neighborhoods: some despise each other across the narrowest of alleys.

Gogol's last words: "A ladder, quick, a ladder!"

"There's nothing new in the world except me," the scornful sum and substance of power.

God quickly gathers up a few stars, so as to save them from us.

The rain makes me as happy as if I had just been born, smoothly and without pain.

Die Zukunft hat sich zu gern, aber es nützt ihr nichts.

Der Sterbende nimmt die Welt mit. Wohin?

Er ist zu alt, um noch einmal auf die Welt zu kommen.

Er hat soviel gepredigt, daß er an nichts mehr glaubt. – Wie sehr darf man seinen Glauben beteuern, ohne ihn zu gefährden? Das *Verhältnis* finden.

Eine Welt, in der jeder noch selber Ahne ist und von niemand abstammt.

Die Klugen klagen sich glücklich.

Du bist zu klug, du mußt mehr *verlieren*. (Rat an einen Freund)

Im Traum: Gedicht aus dem nächsten Jahrhundert.

Geschichte eines Mannes, der an *einem* Worte zugrundegeht.

Er hat sich an den Einteilungen seines Lieblingsphilosophen erhängt.

Seine geheime Sehnsucht: den alten Griechen Wohltaten zu erweisen.

The future likes itself too much—but to no avail.

The dying man takes the world with him. Where to?

He is too old to be born once more.

He has preached so much that he no longer believes in anything. To what extent can one affirm one's faith without endangering it? To find the precise *relation*.

A world in which all are ancestors not descended from anyone.

Wise men mourn merrily.

You are too clever; you have to *lose* more. (Advice to a friend.)

In a dream: a poem from the next century.

The story of a man who is destroyed by *one* word.

He has hanged himself from the categories of his favorite philosopher.

His secret longing: to bestow acts of kindness on the ancient Greeks.

Er macht viel Worte, er vergißt sie, die anderen vergessen sie nicht.

Die Lesenden, die Lesenden überall, auf der ganzen Welt, über den falschen Büchern, eifrig, gläubig, gebückt, vergiftet!

Gedanken, die nie aneinander rühren.

Ein Land, in dem die Ohren gebügelt werden.

Die Entwicklung eines Menschen besteht hauptsächlich aus den Worten, die er sich *abgewöhnt*.

Man müßte sich jahrelang zwingen, nicht weiterzudenken, damit alle zurückgebliebenen Teile der eigenen Person den Vortrupp *einholen*.

Der Respekt, den die Menschen ihren gegenseitigen Gewohnheiten bezeugen, in der Hoffnung, daß die Gewohnheit des einen zu der des anderen stimmt und aus dieser Gemeinsamkeit ein Zeitvertreib erwachsen könnte.

Es will einen ja der Feind nicht *immer* töten. Nur im Paranoiker sieht es so aus, als ob der Mörder immerwährend Mörder wäre.

Er tut solange, was er nicht will, bis er es will: Selbstzerstörung.

He produces a lot of words—which he forgets, but others don't.

Readers, readers everywhere, the world over, bent over the wrong books, eager, gullible, bowed, poisoned!

Thoughts that never touch each other.

A country where ears are being pressed and ironed.

The evolution of a man is measured mainly by the words he has *outgrown*.

One should force oneself to stop thinking for years on end, so that all the parts of one's person which were left behind may *catch up* with the vanguard.

The esteem which people grant their individual customs, in the hope that the customs of one may fit in with those of the other, and so create a common pastime.

After all, your enemy is not *always* intent on killing you. Only to the paranoid mind does it seem as if the murderer were bent on murder at all times.

He does what he doesn't want to do for so long that he finally wants it: self-destruction.

III

Laß die langweiligen, die wirklichen Feinde, erfinde dir lieber welche.

Eine Religion, die Gebete *verbietet*.

Ein Land von Fanatikern, in dem plötzlich jede Meinung erlaubt und geachtet ist.

Es ist etwas Trauriges um unbekleidete Worte, doch ich bin kein Schneider, und lieber als ihnen etwas anzuprobieren, will ich traurig bleiben.

Klarheit und Kürze hindern den Erzähler, denn er lebt von den unberechenbaren Sprüngen der Verwandlung und einem unerschöpflichen Atem.

Man ist oft sehr krank, um sich in jemand anderen zu verwandeln, und wird dann enttäuscht wieder gesund.

Die Form der Organe im Leib eines Menschen drücken sich in seinen Träumen aus, und der Träumer wandelt ahnungslos *in sich* umher.

Er möchte sich das Herz aus der Zukunft reißen.

III

Forget about the real enemies, they're so boring; invent some of your own instead.

A religion which *forbids* prayers.

A country of fanatics in which suddenly every opinion is permitted and respected.

There is something sad about unclothed words, but I'm no tailor and I'd rather stay sad than try to fit them out.

Clarity and concision hamper the storyteller, for he makes his living from unpredictable leaps of transformation and an inexhaustible supply of breath.

A person often falls very ill in order to become someone else and then returns to health much disappointed.

The shapes of our organs often express themselves in our dreams, so that when we dream, we wander *inside ourselves*, entirely unaware.

He would like to tear his heart out of the future.

Es ist schwer, andere zu durchschauen und selber intakt zu bleiben.

Vision der Essenden: Jeder hat eine gefüllte Schüssel vor sich. Keiner hat Hunger, alle sind satt. Jeder greift in die Schüssel des Nachbarn und ißt und ißt.

Ich möchte zu vielen harten Gesichten der Zeit gelangen, wie Quevedo und Goya, und mich so wenig vor mir selber fürchten wie vor ihnen. Ich möchte die Menschen zwingen weiterzuleben, so wenig Aussicht sie darauf haben. Ich möchte zu einer umgekehrten Apokalypse finden, die die Drohung von ihnen *weghebt*. Ich möchte hart sein und hoffen.

Solange es Wissensgebiete gibt, die vom *Experiment* unangetastet bleiben, ist nicht alle Hoffnung vergebens.

Freunde sollten nur die heißen dürfen, die ausfindig machen, wieviel Jahre ihnen bevorstehen und sie dann miteinander ausgleichen.

Seine Urteile sind hauptsächlich Längenmaße.

Es gibt Einsamkeit und Einsamkeit. Der Eine will allein sein, um die anderen alle, die es nicht sind, endlich fühlen zu können. Der Andere will allein sein, weil er so gern der Einzige wäre.

Er vertut seine Zeit nicht, er erwürgt sie, so prall wäre sie, wenn er sie nützen würde.

It is difficult to see through others and still remain intact.

A vision of gluttons: Everyone's plate is full. No one is hungry; all have eaten their fill. Each person digs into his neighbor's plate and eats and eats.

I would like to get to the heart of the many severe and extreme aspects of our time, just like Quevedo and Goya did, unafraid of myself and unafraid of these aspects. I would like to compel people to go on living, however small their chances for survival may be. I would like to arrive at a reverse apocalypse that carries all threats *away*. I would like to be tough, and full of hope.

As long as some domains of science remain untouched by *experimentation*, all hope is not lost.

The only friends worthy of that name are those who find out how many years they still have to live, and then distribute these years equally among one another.

His judgments are merely measures of length.

There is solitude and solitude. One person chooses to be alone so he finally can feel all those who are not. Someone else chooses to be alone just because he so much would like to be the only one.

He doesn't waste his time, he chokes it: that's how tightly filled his time would be if he actually made use of it.

Sehr große Taschen, wie die Handtaschen der Damen, für *Sünden*.

Eine Narbe im Gesicht einer Frau – und schon hat sie die Anziehung des Tieres, das die Wunde gerissen haben könnte.

Viel mehr als Ziele braucht man vor sich, um leben zu können, ein *Gesicht*.

Ein Mensch, der so viele Sprachen kann, daß er immer in der falschen antwortet.

Ein Kopf überm Wasser gab ihm die Kraft der Erzählung wieder.

Man haßt sich nie mehr, als wenn man fühlt, daß man vergeblich sein Bestes hergezeigt hat, und dann, nur dann will man wirklich sterben.

Man braucht eine Unzahl von Gelüsten, denen man nicht nachgibt, sonst wird man, wie schrecklich, zu einem einzigen verzweifelten Hund.

Die tiefste Demütigung der Reichen: daß sie alles *kaufen* können. Sie glauben dann, es ist wirklich alles.

Durch *Vergeßlichkeit* auf eine neue, ganz fremde, herrliche Welt stoßen.

Very large pockets, as big as ladies' handbags, designed for carrying *sins*.

A scar on the face of a woman—and already she has the attraction of the beast which might have torn her flesh.

To live, what you need set out before you—more so than any number of goals—is another *human* face.

A man fluent in so many languages that he always answers in the wrong one.

A head above water restored his storytelling powers.

Never do we hate ourselves more intensely than when we realize we have given our best, yet all in vain. It is then and only then that we truly wish to die.

A person needs an untold number of desires to which he does not yield: otherwise—how terrifying!—he's nothing but a wretched dog.

The greatest humiliation of the rich: that they can *buy* everything. They then believe that that is all there is.

To come upon an entirely alien and beautiful new world as a result of *forgetfulness*.

Er hofft, in allen erregenden Bildern weiterzuleben, die er je gekannt hat.

Ein Ameisen-Streik.

Und wenn die Worte der verschiedenen Sprachen miteinander in geheimer Verbindung stünden?

Ich habe keinen Respekt vor der Wirklichkeit, sobald sie als solche anerkannt ist. Mich interessiert, was ich mit der unerkannten Wirklichkeit mache.

Das Land, in dem man sich schämt, wenn man mit dem Bleistift in der Hand unter Menschen sitzt und ganze Sätze niederschreibt: England. Wären es bloß Zahlen, man wäre keineswegs verdächtig.

Und wenn es doch Geheimnisse *vor Gott* gäbe?

Alle Menschen hätten ein gemeinsames Herz, nicht größer als die Herzen, die wir kennen. Es muß aber die Runde machen, denn wer immer zur Welt kommt, hat ein Anrecht darauf. Die Höhlung für dieses Herz liegt in den Menschen bereit, man hat es nur einzusetzen, und es macht sich sogleich bemerkbar. Die wichtigen und heiligen Sitten hängen mit dem Herzen zusammen. Es ist der größte Augenblick in jedermanns Leben, wenn er das Herz bekommt. Er wird lange darauf vorbereitet, man erzählt ihm, wie selten und alt es ist; wie sonderbar es sich erhalten hat, wie es seine Unverwüstlichkeit eben aus dem Ritus der Einsetzung beziehe. Wäre das Herz lange allein,

He hopes to go on living in all the exciting images he has ever beheld.

Ants on strike.

And what if the words of different languages had some secret connection to one another?

I have no respect for reality as soon as it is acknowledged as such. I am interested in what I can do with unacknowledged reality.

The country where I am ashamed to sit among people, pencil in hand, and write down entire sentences: England. If instead I were to write merely numbers, I would not arouse the slightest suspicion.

And what if, after all, there were secrets *kept from God*?

All human beings would have a single communal heart, no larger than the hearts we know. But that heart has to make the rounds visiting everybody, for everyone alive has a claim on it. To accommodate this heart, all humans are provided with a cavity into which the communal heart is simply placed, whereupon it immediately makes itself felt. All holy rites and important customs are connected to that heart. The receiving of the heart marks the greatest moment in anyone's life. Each person is prepared for it for a long time in advance; he is told how rare and old the heart is; how wonderfully strange it is that it has preserved itself all that time and how it derives its indestructibility precisely from the rite of im-

nicht in einer der unzähligen Höhlungen, die darauf warten, es würde altern, es würde schrumpfen und seine Kraft verlieren. Niemand darf es mehr als einmal in sich haben. Ein Träger reist damit zum nächsten: zweimal hintereinander ist es nicht in derselben Stadt. Der Träger gilt als unverletzlich. Wer wäre so blind, den Träger zu verkennen, er leuchtet, solange er der Glückliche ist. Er weiß zwar, wie wenig er sein Glück verdient, aber das hat nichts zu bedeuten. Diese Auszeichnung kommt ihm wie jedem anderen zu und durch sie erst wird er ein voller Mensch.

Ob einer durch die richtige Auffindung und Aufstellung der Personen, aus denen er besteht, angstlos werden könnte? Er macht sich zu einem Schachspiel und spielt sich remis.

Das Wort Einsamkeit hat einen falschen Ton an sich, als stammte es noch von Gott.

Er kann die bösen Legenden und Geschichten nur ertragen, indem er noch bösere erfindet.

Er sucht verzweifelt nach Leuten, von denen *er nichts weiß*.

Ein Traum
Ein Traum von M., den sie vor Jahren für mich aufgeschrieben hat, ich glaube, es war im Jahre 1942 oder 1943.
»Ich habe unachtsam ein kleines Ding weggeworfen, vielleicht einen Zigarettenstummel. Gleichzeitig wurde mir bewußt – dort liegt ein totes Mädchen – ich sah hin – es war wie unter einem Tisch – oder die Tischplatte bildete ein Dach – ganz vorne waren quer Bretter gelegt, etwa einen halben Me-

plantation. If the heart were left by itself for any length of time, instead of inside one of the innumerable cavities which await it, it would age and shrivel and lose its power. No one is allowed to possess it more than once. One carrier travels with it to the next: the heart never appears in the same town twice in a row. Whoever is carrying the heart is said to be invulnerable—who could be so blind as to mistake the carrier? He is radiant for as long as he is the chosen one. He well knows how little he deserves such good fortune, but that is of no significance. He has as much right as anyone else to this distinction, and only when he has been awarded it does he become a full-fledged human being.

Is it possible for someone to locate and position all the personae he contains in such a way as to lose all fear? He turns himself into a game of chess and plays himself to a draw.

The word "solitude" has a false ring, as if it came straight from God.

The only way he can bear all the evil legends and stories is by inventing even more evil ones.

He is desperately seeking people about whom *he knows nothing*.

A dream:
One of M.'s dreams, which she recorded for me years ago, I believe in 1942 or 1943:
"I threw something away by mistake, it might have been a cigarette butt. At the same time I realized—a dead girl was lying there—I looked over—everything was as if under a table or the tabletop formed a roof—up in the front some boards had been propped up across. They were almost half

ter hoch, so daß man darüber unter den Tisch sehen konnte –
und dort lag sie! *Ganz offen!* – Wenn ich das gewußt hätte,
wäre ich nicht so unachtsam gewesen, einen Stummel dorthin zu werfen – wenn er nur nicht auf sie gefallen ist. – Ich
hatte sie sehr gern. Ich war sehr aufgeregt, daß sie wirklich
ganz offen und sichtbar dort liegt. Als ich mich nieder-
beugte, regte sie sich! Ihr Mund wurde groß und in die
Quere gezogen – ein schwarzes Loch – man wußte nicht, ob
es Lachen oder Schreien war (man konnte keine Zähne sehen), sonst war sie blaßgelb wie getrockneter Teig. Ich war
sehr aufgeregt. ›Also sie wird lebendig. Sie wird vielleicht
wirklich lebendig!‹ Ich hatte sie schrecklich gern. Ich dachte
an C. Wenn das wirklich geschehen würde, daß ich sie lebendig mache!
Ich saß mit ihr. Ich saß ganz nahe bei ihr. Ihre Arme standen
ziemlich gerade herunter. Einer schräg nach links, der andere
nach rechts. Ein Arm von mir war über ihre beiden Arme gelegt. Ich hatte sie furchtbar gern. Ich hatte solche Angst, ich
dachte, es kann nicht wirklich sein, daß sie lebendig wird – sie
wird wieder in den Tod zurückverfallen. Meine Augen fielen
auf ihren einen Arm. Er war aus Ton. Aber frischer, weicher
Ton – man konnte noch so die Spuren einer Spachtel sehen, so
ein paarmal grob heruntergestrichen, und nun kam das Wun-
derbarste! Ich war ihr ganz nahe – meine Augen fielen auf ihre
Backe und ... sie war rosa – weißlich rosa – angehaucht! Da
wußte ich, sie wird lebendig bleiben.«

»Wischnu nahm die Gestalt eines Ebers an und holte die ge-
sunkene Erde aus den Fluten wieder empor. Sie war gesunken,
weil einst Jama auf ihr regierte, unter seiner Regierung aber
Geschöpfe nur geboren wurden und keine starben. Da ward
die Last für die Erde zu groß, und sie sank.«

a yard high, so that one could still see over them and under the table—and there she was! *Entirely exposed!* If I had known that, I would not have been so careless as to throw a cigarette butt over there—I hope it didn't fall right on top of her! I liked her very much. I was greatly upset that she was lying there, really exposed and visible. When I bent down, she started to move! Her mouth grew large and twisted—a black hole—there was no way to tell whether it was laughing or screaming (there were no teeth to be seen). Apart from that, she was a pale yellowish color like dried-up dough. I was very agitated. 'So she's coming to life. Maybe she really will come alive!' I liked her very, very much. I thought of C. If I could really bring her back to life!

"I sat with her. I sat right next to her. Her arms were stretched down fairly straight. One slanted off to the left, the other to the right. One of my own arms was placed over both her arms. I liked her so terribly much. And I was so afraid. I thought it can't be true that she'll return to life— she's bound to fall back into death. I noticed her arm. It was made of clay. But fresh, soft clay, one could still see the traces of the putty knife, a few coarse downward strokes— and now the most wonderful thing occurred! I was right next to her—my eyes came to rest on her cheek and . . . it was pink—a pale pink—as if tinged with the breath of life! And then I knew: she'll stay alive."

"Vishnu took on the form of a boar and fetched the sunken earth back from beneath the flood. It had sunk because once Jama had governed it and under his reign many creatures were born but none died. Thus the burden for the earth became too great and it sank beneath the waters."

In jeder Sprache *ein Wort, das tötet*, das darum nie ausgesprochen wird. Es ist aber allen bekannt, und auf eine geheimnisvolle Weise pflanzt es sich in der Kenntnis der Menschen fort.

Ein Land, in dem jede Frau eine Zeitlang als Kellnerin dient, und jeder Mann als Hund.

Du bist sehr verzweigt, und nur die größten Drohungen können dich zusammenfassen.

Eine sanfte Person, ein sanfter Leib, und darin ein Herz wie das Maul eines Hechtes.

Gott hat sich verlaufen. Jetzt rufen sie ihn von allen Seiten zugleich zurück.

Es ist schon genug, daß ich manchmal, öfters als früher, berechnende Gedanken habe; mehr davon will ich nicht, sonst ist es gleichgültig, daß ich überhaupt lebe. Alles so zu machen wie jeder: einen kleinen Vorteil hier, einen großen dort zu erschnüffeln, zu rechnen, zu jagen, zu greifen – wozu? Ich will daneben leben und nichts *verwenden*.

Wieviel Worte macht ein Mensch und wie wenige sind von ihm.

Diebe, die alles nur für eine bestimmte Zeit stehlen und dann zurückgeben. Das Gefährliche ihres Berufes liegt mehr als im Entwenden im unbemerkten Zurückbringen des Gestohle-

In each language there is *one word that kills* and which, there-fore, is never spoken. But it is known to all and in some mysterious way propagates itself in the minds of humans.

A country in which each woman serves some time as a waitress and each man as a dog.

You are highly ramified and only the most dire threats can keep you together.

A gentle person, with a gentle body, and inside a heart like the maw of a shark.

God has lost His way. And now they are calling Him back from all sides at once.

It is bad enough that I sometimes catch myself—more fre-quently now than in the past—having calculating thoughts; I don't want any more of this, for then it won't matter at all that I am alive. To behave like everyone else, sniffing out a slight advantage here, a larger one over there, counting, pursuing, grabbing—what for? I wish to live on the margin and not *use* anything.

A man produces so many words and creates so few.

Thieves who steal things for a definite time only and then return them. The danger of their profession lies less in the theft than in the unnoticed return of the stolen objects. They

(75)

nen. Ihre Ehre und ihren Stolz legen sie darein, daß dieses gelingt, und ein Gegenstand, den sie länger behalten als sie sich vorgenommen hatten, brennt sie wie die Hölle.

Ein Leben aus versäumten Augenblicken, alle diese Augenblicke leuchten plötzlich *zugleich* auf.

Wechsel der Örtlichkeit, um die Beharrlichkeit des Gedankens zu ertragen.

Gott war lahm und erschuf sich den Menschen als Krücke.

Wo immer er hinkommt, setzt er sich und packt erst einmal seine Überlegenheit aus.

Aus Traurigkeit zu *Zeit* werden.

Er hängt sich das Nichts wie einen Schal um den Hals, doch will und will es ihn nicht erdrosseln.

Abbau des Wissens, ohne Erkenntnisse zu beschädigen.

Ein Tag allein, unter ganz vielen neuen Gesichtern – seine Vorstellung vom Himmelreich.

Nein sagen und die Arme weit öffnen.

feel their pride and honor hinges on this successful return, and any object they keep longer than they intended burns in their hands like hellfire.

A life of wasted moments, moments which suddenly light up *all at once*.

Changing one's location to better bear the permanence of thought.

God was lame and created Man as His crutch.

Wherever he goes, the first thing he does is sit down and unpack his superiority.

To turn into *time*—out of sadness.

He ties nothingness around his neck like a scarf and yet it absolutely refuses to throttle him.

Dismantling knowledge without damaging its component perceptions.

One day all to himself, surrounded by many new faces— his vision of heaven.

To say no with open arms.

Die besten, die wesentlichen Gedanken, die man hat, sind die, die man mit derselben Leidenschaft vergißt, mit der sie sich zuerst gemeldet haben. Als ganz neue Gedanken kommen sie einem dann wieder, in anderen Stationen, man erkennt sie nicht oder nur wie aus einem anderen Leben. Je öfter das geschieht, je mehr solche eigene, aberkannte Leben sie haben, umso bedeutender sind sie.

Gefährlichkeit des wachsenden Mißtrauens: Genugtuung über seine Bewährung. Man ist froh, wenn man recht hatte, das Rechthaben wird zum Wesentlichen. Statt in Verzweiflung zu leben, der einzigen selbstlosen Form des Lebens, gibt man sich mit lächerlichen, belanglosen und nichtigen »Kenntnissen« zufrieden: man ist der Durchschauer, jede Schlechtigkeit hat man vor dem Schlechten selbst gekannt, der sie begeht, und es werden sich immer Schlechtigkeiten finden, die einem nicht gemäß sind, man kann sich ja nicht auf alle selbst einüben. Das Mißtrauen aber wird zu einem kompletten und wohlorganisierten System der Schlechtigkeiten.

Statt Eheringen tragen sie kleine Ehepanzer, über die ganze Länge des Fingers, und schlagen einander damit ins Gesicht.

Der Schmerz macht den Dichter, der voll empfundene, in nichts vermiedene, erkannte, erfaßte, bewahrte Schmerz.

Nietzsche kann mir nie gefährlich werden: denn jenseits von aller Moral ist in mir ein ungeheuer starkes, ein allmächtiges Gefühl von der Heiligkeit jedes, aber auch wirklich jedes Lebens. Daran prallt der roheste wie der raffinierteste Angriff ab. Eher gebe ich mein eigenes Leben ganz und gar auf, als das irgendeines andern auch nur im Prinzip. Kein anderes Gefühl

Our best, our most essential thoughts are those we forget with the same passion with which they revealed themselves in the first place. They then come back as entirely new thoughts, in different situations; we no longer recognize them, or if we do, then only as if they had come from another life. The more this happens, the more of these denied lives such thoughts possess, the more significant they are.

The danger of growing mistrust: the satisfaction of being in the right. Everyone is glad to have been right and being right becomes what is most essential. Instead of living in despair—the only truly selfless way to live—we content ourselves with some ridiculous, irrelevant, and insignificant "insights"; we acquire X-ray vision, we are able to spot every evil deed before the evildoer has committed it, before he's even thought about it. But there will always be evil deeds beyond our scope, nor can we become adept at all of them. Mistrust, however, becomes a complete and well-organized system of evil deeds.

Instead of wedding rings they wear tiny wedding gauntlets extending the whole length of their fingers, and use them to strike each other in the face.

Pain makes the poet, pain fully felt, in no way evaded, pain perceived, grasped, and sustained.

Nietzsche can never become a danger to me: for beyond all moral considerations I feel inside me an enormously powerful, an almighty feeling for the sanctity of every—and I mean literally every—life. And that repels all attacks, from the most simplistic to the most sophisticated. I'd sooner give up my own life than that of anything else alive, even as a matter of principle. No other feeling in me can compare

in mir kommt diesem an Intensität und Unerschütterlichkeit nahe. Ich anerkenne *keinen* Tod. So sind mir alle, die gestorben sind, rechtens noch lebendig, nicht weil sie Forderungen an mich haben, nicht weil ich sie fürchte, nicht weil ich meinen könnte, daß etwas von ihnen noch wirklich lebt, sondern weil sie nie hätten sterben dürfen. Alles Sterben bis jetzt war ein vieltausendfacher Justizmord, den ich nicht legalisieren kann. Was kümmern mich massenhafte Präzedenzfälle, was kümmert mich, daß nicht ein Einziger von immer her lebt! Nietzsches Attacken sind wie eine giftige Luft, aber eine, die mir nichts anhaben kann. Ich atme sie stolz und verächtlich wieder aus und bedaure ihn für die Unsterblichkeit, die seiner wartet.

Plötzlich wurden ihm die Tage kostbar. Er begann sie zu zählen. Seine Eifersucht wandte sich ihnen zu. Es stellte sich heraus, daß sie da besser angebracht ist als bei Menschen.

An jedem langen die Götter *vorbei*, aber manche fühlen sich doch ergriffen.

Er liest über uralte Kriege, als wären Kriege längst abgeschafft.

Taubheit, das größte Glück des Vielredners: er hört sich dann selber nicht mehr.

Kann man denn nie, keinen einzigen Augenblick leben, ohne jemand verabscheuen zu müssen?

with this one in intensity and imperturbability. I do not acknowledge death in *any* form. Thus all who have died are for me still alive, not because they have any claims on me, or because I fear them, or because I might think that some part of them has gone on living, but simply because they never should have died. All the dying up to the present was nothing but judicial murder, carried out thousands and thousands of times and for which I cannot find any legalization. What do I care about the multitude of precedents, what do I care that not one single being has stayed alive since the very beginning! Nietzsche's attacks are like a gust of poisonous air, but one which cannot harm me: I inhale it with pride and exhale it with disdain, and I pity him for the immortality which awaits him.

All of a sudden he felt the days become precious. He started to count them. His jealousy focused on them; and it turned out that they were more fitting objects than people.

The gods reach *past* each and every one of us, and yet some nevertheless feel touched.

He reads about age-old wars, as if wars had been abolished long ago.

Deafness, the greatest fortune that may befall a chatterbox —for then he no longer can hear himself.

Isn't it ever possible to live—be it for just a single instant —without having to despise someone?

Diese sonderbare späte Liebe zu allem Bösen, das einem die nächsten Menschen getan haben, als hätte man es gewollt; als hätte man es darauf und nicht auf das Gute abgesehen gehabt; als wäre das Gute nur ein flüchtiger Nebenzweck der Nähe, und das eigentlich Beständige, die eigentliche Leistung das Böse.

Es strömt soviel Abneigung zwischen ihnen, vom einen zum andern und wieder zurück. Manchmal, um es noch besser zu spüren, sitzen sie Hand in Hand verschränkt. Sie warten auf den gesegneten Augenblick, da ein Schlag, stärker als sie und durch nichts zu beherrschen, sie wie ein Schwert Gottes auseinandertreibt.

Erlösung durch Unbekannte, doch muß es verschiedene Grade der Unbekanntschaft geben: Leute, die einem völlig fremd sind, unheimlich und ganz anders als alles, was man je gesehen hat, andere, die dem Typus, mit dem man umzugehen gewöhnt ist, nicht allzufern sind, andere, die einen in etwas an Menschen erinnern, die man gekannt hat, obwohl man doch sicher weiß, daß sie einem fremd sind, wieder andere, die man vielleicht einmal gesehen hat, und solche, die man bei bestimmten Gelegenheiten trifft, ohne je ein Wort mit ihnen zu wechseln. Solange man ihren Namen nicht kennt, sind sie Unbekannte. Der Name ist die Abwehr der Menschen und mit ihm beginnen sie gegeneinander Schrecken um sich zu verbreiten.
Jeder Grad von Unbekanntheit hat seine eigene Erlösung, und man braucht sie alle. Eine große Kraft der Befreiung kann sich dort gelagert und gesammelt haben, wo man nie nach ihr gesucht hätte, und man vermag nur weiterzuleben, solange man sie überall erwartet.

This strangely belated love for all the evil inflicted by one's nearest and dearest, as if one had willed it to happen, as if one had aimed for that and not for any goodness; as if what was good were merely an ephemeral by-product of proximity, whereas the truly lasting, the essential accomplishment was the evil.

There is such a strong flow of antipathy between them, from one to the other and back again. Sometimes, to feel this with even greater intensity, they sit side by side, hand in hand. They are waiting for the blessed moment when a single blow, more powerful than they and beyond any and all control, will, like the sword of God, split them asunder.

Salvation through unfamiliar people—though there are various degrees of unfamiliarity. Some of these unfamiliar people are completely alien, strange, and totally different from anyone we have ever seen before. Others are not *too* remote from people we are acquainted with, and there are some who may even vaguely remind us of people we have known quite well, although there is no question that they are strangers. Some of these unfamiliar people we may have seen once before and some of them we run into on occasion, without exchanging a single word. As long as we do not know their names, they remain strangers. For names are the armaments of people and it is through names that we spread fear against each other and among ourselves.
Each degree of unfamiliarity has its own salvation, and we need them all. A great power of liberation may have accumulated where we would have expected it least, and it is only the hope of finding it somewhere that enables us to go on living.

IV

Den schweren Himmel, der über ihr lastet, muß man ihr entreißen. Aber wie atmet sie auf, wenn es einem gelingt!

Ein Land, in dem die Leute splitternackt gehen und nur ihre Ohren bedecken. Alle Scham liegt dort in den Ohren.

In einem Traum bringt er Fünflinge zur Welt, und alle sind lesbar.

Noch nie, seit ich denken kann, habe ich zu jemand Herr! gesagt, und wie leicht ist es Herr! zu sagen und wie groß die Versuchung. Hundert Göttern bin ich genaht, und jedem sah ich klar und mit Haß für den Tod der Menschen ins Gesicht.

Man muß sich für Liebe oder für Gerechtigkeit entscheiden. Ich kann es nicht, ich will beides.

Die Diebin, die immer daran denken muß, daß sie ihr *Gesicht* gestohlen hat.

Wie soll man sie ertragen, diese Mit-Paranoiker, die genau so funktionieren wie man selbst, deren winzigste Regung man zum voraus begreift, in denen man vorausahnt, was noch kommen könnte, die einen in jeder Kleinigkeit, erschreckend präzis, spiegeln, und während alles formal so stimmt, ist der ganze Inhalt verschieden!

IV

The skies that weigh so heavily upon her must be torn from her shoulders. But how she will sigh with relief if someone actually succeeds in so doing!

A country in which the people go around stark naked and only cover their ears. In that land all shame resides in the ears.

In a dream he bears quintuplets, all of them legible.

For as long as I can remember I have never called anyone "Lord!"—though it is very easy to say "Lord!" and very tempting. I have approached hundreds of gods and looked each of them straight in the eye, full of hatred, all on account of men's mortality.

People must decide between love and justice. I cannot, because I want both.

The female thief who can never escape the thought that she has stolen her *face*.

How am I to tolerate those fellow paranoiacs, who function in exactly the same way as I do, whose tiniest impulses I understand in advance, who allow me to anticipate what may still happen, who mirror my own self in every detail and with terrifying accuracy—and though the form fits perfectly, the content is totally different!

Von Nebel zu Nebel größere Klarheit, bis er im Nebel der höchsten Klarheit ganz aufgeht und verschwindet.

Diese Fahrzeuge im Nebel, große, kleine, von Menschen bis zu Lastwagen, gleiten alle an ihm vorüber, ohne sich zu stoßen. Sie berühren nicht, sie streicheln einander, es streitet nichts, für alles ist Platz. Die Vorsicht, mit der man einander begegnet, die liebevolle Behutsamkeit, und wer dann doch aufeinander stößt, empfindet es als eine Offenbarung. Der Nebel in dieser Stadt ist das Bild paradiesischen Friedens, des einzigen, der hier möglich ist, und erfüllt den Beschauer mit unendlichem Glücksgefühl.

Der Menschenhasser: er hungert acht Tage und ißt dann allein.

Verwirrende Vorstellung: daß die Unsterblichkeit erst an einem Haustier gelingt, an einem Hund z. B.: der unsterbliche Hund.

Es ist nicht das Alleinsein, das ich zu erlernen habe, denn es fällt mir nicht schwer, ich bin gern allein; es ist das *Schweigen* unter Menschen. Diese plötzlichen Ausbrüche von raschen, heftigen Reden sind wertlos und verwirrend. Es ist gar nicht so wichtig, an wen sie gerichtet sind, ob man mich versteht oder nicht; die Worte selbst, meine eigenen Worte haben eine furchtbare und verheerende Wirkung auf mich. Sie sind zu stark, ich muß sie dämpfen, indem ich sie niederschreibe. Was ich rede, ist so heftig, daß jeder, der es hört, ausweichen muß, schon um sich selbst vor mir zu bewahren. Ich aber kann meinen Worten nicht ausweichen; ich bin ihnen ausgeliefert; ich nehme sie ganz auf, ich verstehe sie ganz, ich gerate durch sie in Erregung wie ein Meer im Sturm.

He passes from fog to fog, finding greater and greater clarity, until he completely dissolves in the fog of greatest clarity, and disappears.

These vehicles in the fog, large and small, from people to trucks, all glide by him without bumping into each other. They do not touch but do exchange caresses, there are no quarrels, there's room for everything. The caution, the gentle carefulness with which each encounters the other— and when a collision nevertheless occurs it is perceived as a revelation. The fog in this city is the very picture of paradisiac peace, the only peace possible here, and it fills the observer with a feeling of infinite bliss.

The misanthrope: he fasts for eight days and then eats all alone.

A confusing notion: what if immortality were first accomplished by a pet, for instance by a dog: the immortal dog.

It isn't being alone that I need to learn, for that comes easy to me. I like being alone; what I need to learn is how to *keep silent* among people. These abrupt outbursts of fast and furious talk are worthless and confusing. It doesn't really matter to whom my words are addressed or whether or not they are understood; the words in themselves, my own words, have a horrifying and devastating effect on me. They are too strong; I need to muffle them by writing them down. What I say to others is so violent that whoever hears it has to get out of the way, so as to protect himself somehow from my eruptions. But I myself cannot evade my words; I am at their mercy; I take them in whole; I understand them fully and they shake me the way a storm shakes up the sea.

Jedes Wort hat seine Opfer, auf die es mit Gewalt wirkt; manchmal glaube ich, daß ich aller Worte Opfer bin. Ich kann nur denen entkommen, die ich niederschreibe; diese beruhigen mich; diese scheinen mir erlaubt; von ihnen bin ich überzeugt, daß sie mich einmal, wenn ich tot bin, nicht mehr erregen werden, obwohl sie auch dann noch, dann erst recht, da sind.

Schmeichel-Diebe: sie sagen einem die herrlichsten Dinge über alles, was sie unterdessen in den Taschen finden.

Wheen, den ich sehr mag, Bibliothekar am Victoria and Albert Museum, erzählte mir heute von der ersten Demütigung, deren er sich aus seiner Kindheit erinnert. Er wuchs in Australien auf, in Sidney, wo er nie mit Eingeborenen zusammenkam. Eines Tages, er mochte damals acht Jahre zählen, machte die ganze Klasse mit dem Lehrer einen Ausflug nach Botany Bay, wo es ein Reservat von Eingeborenen gab. Sie führten da ein sehr elendes Leben im größten Schmutz und tranken sich zu Tod. Der Lehrer führte sie zu einem alten Manne, der da als eine Art Häuptling eingesetzt war. Er lag im Eingang einer Höhle und drehte sich, als er der Kinder ansichtig wurde, weg. Der Lehrer gab sich Mühe, ihn zu überreden, er solle doch zu ihnen sprechen, sie seien gekommen, ihn zu sehen. Der Alte warf einen Blick auf den kleinen Wheen und zeigte einen solchen Widerwillen vor ihm, wie der es noch nie erlebt hatte. Dann drehte der Alte sich wieder weg und war durch nichts mehr zu bewegen, seine Lage zu verändern. Der Ekel, den er gezeigt hatte, war etwas, das Wheen nie mehr vergaß. Sein ganzes späteres Leben kam er sich unerwünscht und verabscheut vor.
Als er später, ein junger Mann, nach Europa fuhr, stieg er in Suez von Bord und ging mit einem jungen Mädchen ins Eingeborenen-Viertel. Ein Eingeborener mit sehr schönem, stolzen

Each word has its own victims upon which it acts violently; sometimes I believe that I am the victim of all words. I can only escape from those I write down; those pacify me; they seem permissible to me; and I am convinced that once I am dead, they will no longer disturb me, even though they will be there still—in fact, that is when they truly will begin to exist.

Flatterer-thieves: they tell you the most delightful things about whatever they're in the process of filching from your pockets.

Wheen, librarian at the Victoria and Albert Museum, whom I like very much, today told me about the first humiliating experience he remembers from his childhood. He grew up in Australia, in Sydney, where he never had any contacts with the aboriginals. One day, when he was about eight years old, his whole class was taken by their teacher on an excursion to Botany Bay, where a reservation was located. The people there led a miserable existence in the worst of squalor and regularly drank themselves to death. The teacher brought them to an old man who had been appointed a kind of chieftain of the reservation. He was lying at the entrance to a cave, and upon seeing the group of children, simply turned his back to them. The teacher tried hard to persuade him to speak to the children, who had come especially to see him. The old man glanced at little Wheen with such revulsion in his eyes as the boy had never seen. Then the old man turned away once more and nothing could move him to change his position. But the disgust he had shown Wheen on that occasion was something Wheen was never able to forget. All during his later life he felt unwanted and despised.
When later, as a young man en route to Europe, he went ashore at Suez and, accompanied by a young girl, visited the old quarter, a Suez native with a proud and very hand-

Gesicht kam ihnen entgegen und spuckte Wheen ohne jede Veranlassung ins Gesicht. Wir sprachen von anderen Dingen, und erst später fragte ich ihn, was er darauf getan hatte. Er habe nicht zurückgeschlagen und sich sehr elend danach gefühlt, ganz besonders aber das junge Mädchen, das von ihm diese normale Reaktion erwartet habe. Er erklärte sein Verhalten durch Feigheit, und in einer ausführlichen Diskussion, die wir darüber hatten, war er von diesem Wort nicht abzubringen. Als wir uns eine Stunde später trennten, fragte er mich plötzlich, ob ich mich nie dafür geschämt hätte, ein Weißer zu sein.

Sie lächelt seine Worte an wie Ballons und weiß nicht, wie leicht und wie freudig sie platzen.

Was kann man? Was kann man nicht? Er kann alle verhungern lassen, aber er kann niemand töten.

Der Fremdmacher geht zwischen den Leuten umher und schiebt sie auseinander.

Es belustigt mich, wenn Unbekannte neben mir, die mich überhaupt nicht kennen, über mich spotten. Es macht mich übermütig, sie zu hören und zu verstehen, was sie in einer Sprache, die sie für unverständlich halten, gegen mich sagen. Ich habe dann das Gefühl, daß ich in einer falschen Haut dasitze, und über diese sprechen und urteilen sie. Darunter aber bin ich selbst, und wie vieles *Richtige* könnte ich ihnen über sie selber sagen.

In der Kindheit so gut genährt werden, daß man nie wieder zu essen braucht.

some face came toward them and, without the slightest provocation, spat straight into Wheen's face. — We then spoke of other things and it was only later that I asked Wheen how he had reacted. He had not hit the man in return and had felt very bad about that in retrospect, particularly since the young girl had expected such a reaction from him as normal. He explained his behavior as mere cowardice, and in a long discussion which then ensued, could not be dissuaded from using this word. When we parted an hour later, he suddenly asked me whether I had ever been ashamed of being a white man.

She smiles at his words as if they were balloons—unaware how readily and joyfully they burst.

What is one capable of? What is one incapable of? One man is capable of letting everyone starve to death, but he cannot kill anybody.

The *alienator* goes among the people, pushing them apart.

It amuses me when people who do not know me at all make fun of me in my presence. I am overjoyed to hear and understand what they are saying about me in a language they think I do not understand. I then have the feeling that I'm sitting there clad in a false skin and that it is that skin they are discussing and judging. But underneath I am myself, and how many *true things* could I tell them about themselves!

To be so well fed as a child that one never need eat again.

Es quält ihn der Gedanke, daß vielleicht jeder *zu spät* gestorben ist und unser Tod nur durch seine Verschiebung ganz Tod ist; daß jeder die Möglichkeit hätte weiterzuleben, wenn er *rechtzeitig* stürbe, aber keiner weiß wann.

Alle Liebhaber des Todes enden damit, daß sie ihn wegleugnen.

Das Mädchen, das sich nur unter einem Kometen entkleidet.

Sie setzt sich jedem ersten besten Stuhl auf den Schoß.

Die Zeit hat ihren mütterlichen Stolz, sie will erfüllt und nicht zerschnitten werden.

Gottes Herzschlag in uns: die Angst.

Das Interesse für Preise, als würde man sich an ihnen festhalten. Die besten Freunde hier halten sich Preise zum Abschied entgegen wie Hände: soviel für dich, soviel für mich, je genauer, umso bessere Freunde sind sie.

Er kann jedem helfen, wenn er nichts dafür bekommt.

Sie durchwandert die ganze Erde nach seiner verlorenen Eifersucht.

Das Echo seiner Kindheit ist verstimmt.

He is tormented by the idea that perhaps everyone died *too late* and that it is this delay alone that makes our dying a genuine death; anyone could go on living if he only were to die *at the right moment*, but no one knows when that is.

All lovers of death end up disavowing it.

The girl who only takes off her clothes under a comet.

She sits down in the lap of the first chair that comes her way.

Time has its maternal pride: it wants to be fulfilled and not sliced up.

God's heartbeat in us: fear.

The interest in numbers as if one could hang on to them. Here best friends offer numbers in farewell as if these were hands: so much for me; so much for you; the more exact the exchange, the better friends they are.

He can help anyone as long as he doesn't receive anything in return.

She travels the whole wide world in search of his lost jealousy.

The echo of his childhood is out of tune.

Dieser Tanz der Kraniche – wie erfrechen sich Menschen noch, einen Schritt zu tun!

Sein Menschenhaß kam nur seiner Menschenliebe gleich.

Du verbindest so rasch, daß du zu wenig vergleichst. Sind es nur die Sammler, die vergleichen?

Die einzigen Menschen, die ich langweilig finde, sind Verwandte.

Sein Traum: daß die Namen allein leben und alles Lebende ist nur ein Traum der Namen.

Noch immer hast du es nicht gelernt, den Augenblick in seiner Kraft zu fassen: du meinst, er wird weiterleuchten, du erkennst ihn nicht als Augenblick; du glaubst, ein neues Wort kann nicht erlöschen. Sie erlöschen aber alle, es ist nur da, was du wirklich im Augenblick niederschreibst. Diese eine Beschränkung wirst du anerkennen müssen oder du versäumst dein eigentliches Leben, das der Gedanken.

Wieviele Hände fahren gleichzeitig überallhin aus! Deine Ehrfurcht gilt einer einzigen Hand.

Sie hat seine Unsterblichkeit aufgegessen.

Ich habe das Erkennen satt, die Beziehungen zu allem Früheren, die Verbindungen, Fortsetzungen, Verkleidungen, Ent-

The dance of the cranes! Seeing it, how can humans still dare to take even a single step?

His misanthropy was rivaled only by his love of mankind.

You connect so quickly that you compare too little. Perhaps only those who collect can really compare.

The only people I find boring are relatives.

His dream: Only the names are alive—and all life is merely *their* dream.

You still have not learned to grasp the moment at the height of its power: you think it will continue shining, you don't recognize it as a moment in time; you believe a new word cannot expire. But they all expire, and the only thing that continues to exist is what you write down at that moment. You shall have to recognize this limitation, otherwise you will miss out on your true life, that of your thoughts.

How numerous the hands flying out to all points at the same time! And yet you revere only one.

She has devoured his immortality.

I'm sick of all perception, of the connections to all that has been before, the interrelations, the follow-ups, the disguises,

hüllungen, ich möchte etwas erleben, das mit nichts zusammenhängt, was in mir früher da war, und das sich nicht fortsetzt und nicht zum Bleiben verurteilt ist; etwas mit raschen, abrupten Bewegungen, die nie berechenbar sind, ich möchte mit einem Wort ein Wunder.

Die Einsamkeit der Schmerzen: wie sonderbar, daß die Menschen einander nicht mehr dafür grollen!

Die emphatischen Worte ausmerzen. Der Gedanke selbst sei stark und nicht der Affekt, mit dem du ihn ausdrückst.

Diese erwartungsvolle Ermüdung durch viele neue Gesichter, sei es, daß sie um einen herum sitzen, sei es, daß sie einem entgegenkommen, und das nie zu stillende Bedürfnis nach eben dieser Ermüdung! Nichts macht den modernen Menschen so sehr aus, wie diese besondere Art von Fluidität und Dichte, in die man täglich mehrmals taucht, um sich täglich mehrmals wieder von ihr zu lösen.

An der Vorstellung des Jüngsten Gerichts ist für mich hinreißend die Auferstehung aller *Leiber*, ihr Wiederzusammenfinden.

Länder, die zum Hineinwerfen da sind, wie Amerika, und solche zum Hinauswerfen: England.

Diese Familien! Eine wie die andere, und jede so stolz auf sich!

the revelations; I wish to experience something which has no relation to anything that was in me earlier, something which does not reproduce itself and is not doomed to stay; something with swift, abrupt motions, never predictable—in a word, I wish for a miracle.

The loneliness of pain: how strange that humans should not resent each other for it more than they do.

Weed out the emphatic words. Let the thought itself be powerful and not the emotion with which you express it.

This anxious fatigue caused by many new faces, whether they are sitting around you or coming toward you, and the unquenchable need for precisely that fatigue! Nothing epitomizes modern man as much as this special combination of fluidity and density into which he plunges several times each day, only to detach himself again from it every time.

I am fascinated by the notion in the Last Judgment of the resurrection of all *bodies*, their reassemblement.

Countries made for throwing things in, such as America, and for throwing things out: England.

Those families! All exactly alike, and each so proud of itself.

Der Glücklichste: er kennt alle und niemand kennt ihn.

Es ist herrlich, ein Narr zu sein, wenn man klug ist.

Sein Leben ist eine Suche nach allen Unverkäuflichkeiten.

Laß jeden reden; du rede nicht: deine Worte nehmen den Menschen ihre Gestalt. Deine Begeisterung verwischt ihre Grenzen; sie kennen sich selber nicht mehr, wenn du sprichst; sie sind *du*.

Er fühlt sich so einsam, daß er darum bettelt, Ratschläge erteilen zu dürfen.

Immer wenn er nichts zu sagen hat, erwähnt er Gott.

Es war alles zu früh belebt, so hat sich der Mensch auf der Erde *eingetötet*, bevor er noch etwas wußte.

Manche Worte sind so vielsinnig, daß es um ihrer Kenntnis willen allein verlohnt, gelebt zu haben.

Er hat niemand, den er um Gnade bitten könnte. Der stolze Glaubenslose!
Er kann vor niemand niederknien: sein Kreuz.

The happiest man: he knows everybody and no one knows him.

It is wonderful to be a fool if one is wise.

His life is a search for everything that can't be sold.

Let all others speak; but you yourself refrain: your words rob people of their shape. Your enthusiasm blurs their outlines; when you speak, they no longer know themselves; they become *you*.

He feels so lonely that he begs for permission to give advice.

Whenever he has nothing to say he mentions God.

Everything came alive too soon, so that mankind became *used to death* long before knowing better.

Some words are so manifold in meaning that merely to have known them makes having lived worthwhile.

He has no one to implore for mercy. The proud unbeliever! He cannot kneel to anyone: this is his cross.

Stolz bezahlt sich am höchsten, heiter der Wurm, der keinen hat.

Du hast dich so sehr ausgebreitet, du kannst die Herde deiner Gedanken nicht übersehen und du willst sie noch immer nicht zähmen.

Ein Lächeln, das den Tod *aufhält*.

Ahnungslose Vermehrer.

Hätte er nur mehr gelesen, dann wüßte er wirklich nichts. Aber dieses bißchen Wissen, das aus seinen Lücken Zutrauen bezieht, ist trügerisch und gefährlich.

Du bist so schön, sagt er manchmal, und niemand ist da, dem er es sagt.

Ich bin in ein Labyrinth der merkwürdigsten Gedanken geraten, vielleicht weil ich mich nicht davor gescheut habe, mich dieser Zeit zu stellen, vielleicht aus Prahlerei, einer Art jugendlicher Überzeugung, daß selbst sie geistig zu bewältigen wäre, aber was immer der Grund – jetzt ist das Labyrinth da, und ich bin mitten darin und ich muß anderen wie mir selbst einen Weg hinaus zeigen.

Vergiß nicht, daß du für manche so dumm bist, wie der Dümmste für dich.

Pride commands the highest price; happy the worm who has none.

You have spread yourself so thin that you no longer can oversee the whole herd of your thoughts; nevertheless, you still don't want to tame them.

A smile that *staves off* death.

Unwitting propagators.

If only he had read more, then he really would know nothing at all. But this little bit of knowledge that draws confidence from its gaps is deceptive and pernicious.

You are so beautiful, he says at times—but he is speaking to no one.

I have become lost in a labyrinth of the strangest thoughts, perhaps because I was not afraid of confronting these times, perhaps out of boastfulness, a kind of youthful conviction that they, too, could be mastered spiritually—but whatever the reason, the labyrinth is there, I am caught in the middle of it, and I have to find some way out, for others as well as for myself.

Don't forget that for some you are just as stupid as the most stupid is for you.

Ein Park in London: viele und unbekannte Menschen, nicht zu nah, nicht zu fern, alle im milden Licht des Spätsommers, solche die liegen, solche die stehen, Sitzende, Gehende, alle am Leben unter einem warmen Himmel, niemand schreit, niemand streitet, jeder kommt und geht frei, allein, mit andern, mit wem er will, und solange er bleibt, ist niemand durch ihn beengt oder traurig. Es ist, als könnten die Menschen ins Paradies, ohne darin bleiben zu müssen und als würden sie für keine Sünde je daraus verstoßen.

Es scheint mir, daß ohne eine neue Einstellung zum Tode über das Leben nichts wirklich zu sagen ist.
Das Dasein will überall sein, sonst ist es kein Dasein.
Ich anerkenne keinen einzigen Tod. Daß auch Mücken und Flöhe sterben, macht mir den Tod nicht begreiflicher als die furchtbare Geschichte von der Erbsünde.
Es macht keinen Unterschied, ob etwas von uns noch irgendwo weiter besteht oder nicht. Wir leben hier nicht genug. Wir haben keine Zeit, uns hier zu bewähren. Und da wir den Tod anerkennen, verwenden wir ihn.
Wie sollte es keine Mörder geben, solange es dem Menschen *gemäß* ist zu sterben, solange er sich nicht dafür schämt, solange er den Tod in seine Institutionen *eingebaut* hat, als wäre er ihr sicheres, bestes und sinnvollstes Fundament? –

Die anscheinende Zweckmäßigkeit der Organismen hat uns am meisten irregeführt.

Die massa damnata des Augustin ist das römische Erbteil der *Schlacht*.

A park in London: many people, strangers, not too close and not too far off, all of them in the mild light of late summer, some lying down, some standing, some sitting or walking, all alive beneath a warm sky, no one is shouting, no one is fighting, everyone comes and goes freely, alone or with others, with whomever he pleases, and everyone can stay as long as he wants without making anyone feel oppressed or saddened. It is as if people were free to enter paradise with no obligation to remain there and no danger of being expelled for any sin whatsoever.

It seems to me that without a new attitude toward death nothing worthwhile can be said regarding life.
Life seeks to be everywhere, otherwise it is not life.
I do not acknowledge any kind of death. That gnats and fleas also die does not make death any more comprehensible to me than the horrifying story of the Original Sin.
It makes no difference whether or not any part of us continues to exist somewhere else. We don't live enough here, on earth. We don't have enough time to prove ourselves here. And since we acknowledge death, we use it.
Why shouldn't there be any murderers when we consider it *fitting* for people to die, when we are not ashamed of it, when we have *incorporated* death into our institutions, as if it were their best, their most solid and meaningful foundation?

It is the apparent expediency of organisms which has led us most astray.

The Augustinian *massa damnata* is the Roman legacy inherited from battle.

Wer den Eigen-Jammer zu sehr verachtet, fühlt auch den fremden nicht mehr. *Stoiker*

Die wahren Dinge, die ich von mir erzähle, kommen mir am ehesten wie Lügen vor.

Andere Herzen einsetzen, statt von Hyänen die von Pferden.

Es wäre besser, wenn alle Götter bloß ausgewandert wären und man sie auf einem anderen Sterne wiederfände.

Ich hasse die Geschichte; ich lese nichts lieber; ich schulde ihr alles.

Eine Peterskirche voller Päpste.

N. will jede Berührung rückgängig machen, sobald er erfährt, daß jemand tot ist. Er fürchtet eine nachträgliche Ansteckung durch den Tod. Er glaubt, am Leben bleiben zu können, wenn er die Toten wirksam, auch in sich wirksam verleugnet. Um den Tod zu vermeiden, bringt er seine Toten ganz um.

Händler aus Versöhnlichkeit. Händler aus Zanksucht.

Grade der Verzweiflung: sich an nichts erinnern, an manches, an alles.

Whoever despises his own misery excessively no longer feels
that of others. *From the Stoics*

The things I tell about myself that are true seem most like
lies to me.

To implant other hearts: horses as donors instead of hyenas.

It would be better if all the gods had simply emigrated and
we could meet them on another star.

I hate history; there is nothing I'd rather read; I owe everything to it.

A St. Peter's Basilica full of popes.

N. wishes to cancel retroactively all contact with someone
as soon as he knows that that someone has died. He fears a
delayed contamination by death. He believes he can go on
living for as long as he effectively denies—also within
himself—those who have died. To avoid death, he kills his
own dead even more thoroughly.

Some haggle because they are conciliatory, others because
they are cantankerous.

Degrees of despair: to remember nothing at all; to remember
some things; to remember everything.

Bei verschiedenem Lichte denken. Die unleserlichen Philosophen unterwerfen sich keiner Änderung ihres Lichts.

Der Turm von Babel aus *Knochen*, und alle Sprachen verlernt.

Jedes Gespräch regt ihn furchtbar auf, nach einem Jahr.

Der Glückliche, dessen Bedenken sich *betrinken*.

Sie empfängt und verabschiedet ihn mit Tränen; sie gibt ihm Tränen zu essen. Sie zieht ihm Tränen an. Sie liest ihm Tränen vor.

Die Gebete, mit denen sie sich Gott entziehen.

Bei diesem Volk wird das Geld vom König rein geleckt.

Zwangsweise Namensänderung alle fünf Jahre. Das Schicksal der Berühmten. Ihre Schwindeleien.

Die diabolische Freude der Toten, weil wir nichts über sie wissen.

Die ›Elektra‹ *des Sophokles* enthält den Tod in jeder Form. Sie steht im Schatten eines Mordes und führt zu zwei weiteren. Es sind Morde in konzentriertester Form, der erste an einem Gatten, Agamemnon, an einer Mutter, Klytämnestra, der

To think by different lights. The unreadable philosophers do not submit to any changes in their light.

The Tower of Babel made of *bones*, and all languages forgotten.

Each conversation makes him terribly upset—a year later.

The happy man whose misgivings *drink themselves into a stupor*.

She receives him with tears and bids him farewell with tears: she gives him tears to eat. She clothes him in tears. And when she reads to him out loud, she reads tears.

The prayers with which they evade God.

The nation's lucre is licked clean by its king.

Compulsory change of name every five years. The fate of celebrities. Their frauds.

The diabolic joy of the dead because we know nothing of them.

The *Electra* of Sophocles contains death in all its forms. The heroine stands in the shadow of one murder and leads to two others. These are murders in their most concentrated form, the first one that of a husband, Agamemnon, the second one that of a mother, Clytemnestra. Only the third

zweite. Nur der dritte, letzte ist der Mord an einem Liebhaber, der kein naher Blutsverwandter ist. Elektra ist immer vom Gedanken an den Tod ihres Vaters erfüllt. Ihr Bruder, Orestes, den sie zum Rächer bestellt hat, lebt in einer anderen Stadt; er ist immer in Verbindung mit ihr. Jetzt, da er endlich anlangt, läßt er die Nachricht von seinem eigenen Tod verbreiten. Man erlebt die Wirkung dieser Nachricht auf Klytämnestra und Elektra zugleich. Der Bote schildert in sehr beredter Weise des Orestes Sturz bei einem Wagenrennen. Für die Mutter, die ihn als Rächer fürchtet, ist es der am meisten *gewünschte* Tod, für die Schwester, die ihre ganze Hoffnung auf Orest gesetzt hat, ist es der Tod, den sie am meisten *fürchtet*. Er selbst erscheint, nachdem die Mutter Elektra verlassen hat, als Überbringer seiner eigenen Asche. So erlebt er den Schmerz der Schwester um seinen Tod, etwas was Sterblichen selten vergönnt ist; denn eben bei einer solchen Nachricht sind sie nie zugegen. Elektras Schmerz ist so groß, daß Orestes sich offenbart: für sie kehrt er zum Leben zurück. Ihre Wiederbegegnung ist um die falsche Nachricht intensiver.

In einer Szene zuvor hat Elektra das Amt des Rächers auf sich genommen, da sie ihren Bruder tot glaubt. Ihre Schwester, die sie zur Hilfe bereden wollte, hat dieses Amt abgelehnt. Sobald Orestes lebt, ist *er* wieder der Rächer. Als Bote und Träger seiner eigenen Asche geht er in den Palast hinein zu seiner Mutter und erschlägt sie. Elektra, draußen, schlägt mit, durch ihren furchtbaren Satz.

Der Schluß, die Ermordung des Aigisthos, wird zu einer neuen Verwandlung des Todes verwendet. Eine Bahre mit einer verhüllten Leiche wird ihm vorgeführt: er glaubt, der tote Orest ist darunter; er hebt das Tuch und sieht Klytämnestra blutig vor sich.

So sind in diesem Stück *alle* Elemente des Sterbens und des Todes enthalten. Das *Andenken* an die tote Tochter, das Klytämnestra beseelt – sie hat Iphigenie an Agamemnon gerächt –; das Andenken an den toten Vater: als Rachewille bei Elektra und Orest, als Ergebung in den Tod bei ihrer Schwester Chry-

and last murder is that of a lover, who is not a close blood relative. Electra is filled with thoughts of her father's death at all times. Her brother, Orestes, whom she has appointed her avenger, lives in another town, but is in constant touch with her. Now that he is finally about to arrive, he spreads the news of his own death. We simultaneously experience Clytemnestra's and Electra's reaction to the news. The messenger describes with great eloquence the death of Orestes in a fall during a chariot race. For the mother, who fears him as avenger, it is the death *most wished for*; for the sister, who had set all her hopes on Orestes, it is the death *most dreaded*. After her mother has left Electra, Orestes appears disguised as the bearer of his own ashes. In this way he witnesses his sister's grief over his own death, a spectacle rarely granted to mortals since they are never present when such tidings arrive. Electra's suffering is so great that Orestes reveals himself to her: for her sake he returns to the living. Their reunion is all the more intense as a result of the earlier false news of his death.

In a preceding scene Electra herself had assumed the role of avenger since she thought her brother dead. Her sister, whom she had attempted to enlist in this endeavor, had refused her. As soon as Orestes returns to life, *he* once again becomes the avenger. As messenger and bearer of his own ashes he enters the palace and slays his mother. Outside, Electra, for her part, strikes at her mother with her terrible sentence, and so joins in the slaying.

The end, the murder of Aegisthus, provides a new variation on death: Aegisthus is shown a bier with a shrouded corpse he believes to be the dead Orestes; he lifts the cloth and is confronted instead with the bloodied body of Clytemnestra. This play thus contains *all* the elements of death and dying. The *memory* of the dead daughter which inspires Clytemnestra—she avenged Iphigenia's death by murdering Agamemnon; the memory of the dead father which prompts the avenging urge in Electra and Orestes, and the submission to death in Electra's sister Chrisotemis; the *fear* of death in

sothemis; die *Angst* vor dem Tod, bei den Schuldigen, bei Klytämnestra und anders bei Aigisthos, der die Augenblicke, bevor er gefällt wird, *bewußt* erlebt. Die *Unerschrockenheit* vor dem Tod bei Elektra und ihre faszinierende Wirkung auf andere. Der Mörder, der sich als Toter verstellt und mit seiner eigenen Asche ankommt. Die Bahre, die Urne mit Asche, das Totenopfer. Die Todesnachricht und ihre sehr verschieden geartete Wirkung. Das Umschlagen von einem gewünschten Tod in den eigenen (bei Klytämnestra), dasselbe Umschlagen, langsamer, von einem gewünschten Tod in einen gefürchteten und schließlich in den eigenen (bei Aigisthos: Orest – Klytämnestra – er selbst). Alle diese Formen, Elemente, Verwandlungen des Todes werden vom Chor miterlebt. Seine Funktion ist die eines Massenkristalls, der die Vorgänge für die größere Zuhörerschaft polarisiert. Orestes erscheint mit einem Freund, der nie spricht und als sein Doppelgänger oder Schatten wirkt. Der Bote, ein sehr alter Mann, ist etwas wie ein tückischer Todesengel, durch die Nachricht von einem falschen Tod bereitet er einen wahren vor. (1951)

Sie kann nur lieben, wenn man sie für eine andere hält.

Freude an Preissteigerungen: Er wandert durch die Straßen der Stadt, sieht in jedes Schaufenster und ist glücklich, weil alles teurer geworden ist. Gegenstände, die ihm früher gleichgültig waren, reizen ihn jetzt zum Kauf. Er ist besorgt, daß alles plötzlich billiger werden könnte, bevor er genug teuer eingekauft hat. Er lächelt den Verkäufern zu, die sich schämen möchten und alle entweder schuldig oder unverschämt dreinblicken. Er muntert sie auf: nur höher! höher! Könnte ich nicht dasselbe teurer haben? Aber sie mißverstehen ihn und meinen, er will eine bessere Qualität. Er möchte gegenwärtig sein, wenn Preise in die Höhe gehen; immer geschieht es hinter seinem Rücken, nachts, wenn die Läden geschlossen sind.

the guilty ones, in Clytemnestra and, in a different manner, in Aegisthus, who experiences the moments before he is slain in *full consciousness*. Electra's own *fearlessness* in the face of death and its spellbinding effect on others. The murderer who presents himself as a dead man and who arrives bearing his own ashes. The bier, the urn filled with ashes, the sacrifice for the dead. The news of a death and its extremely varied effect on all others. The inversion of a wished-for death into that of the wish-bearer (Clytemnestra); the same inversion, albeit a slower one, from a wished-for death into a feared death and, ultimately, into one's own (Aegisthus: Orestes–Clytemnestra–himself). All these different forms, elements, and transformations of death are also experienced by the chorus. Its function is that of a huge crystal which polarizes the events for the larger audience. Orestes appears with a friend who never speaks and seems to be his double or his shadow. The messenger, a very old man, is a bit like an insidious angel of death: in delivering the news of a false death, he prepares the way for a real one. (1951)

She can love only if mistaken for another.

Pleasure in price increases: He strolls through the streets of the city, looks into all the shop windows, and is happy because everything has become more expensive. Items he once treated with indifference now tempt him as potential purchases. He's worried that everything might become cheaper before he has bought enough at high prices. He smiles at the salespeople, who are all somewhat ashamed and look at everyone either a bit guiltily or brazenly impertinent. He encourages them: Higher! Higher! But they misunderstand him, thinking that what he wants is higher quality. He would like to be present when prices go up; but it always occurs behind his back, at night, when the shops are closed.

V

Die Verantwortung des Stummen. Ein Roman.

Sie will sich umbringen, sagt sie, aber erst nachdem er sich bei ihr entschuldigt hat.

Es gibt eine leuchtende und eine bittere Angst. Die erste wächst und wächst und dehnt sich solange aus, bis sie birst. Die zweite schrumpft ein und vertrocknet. Diese bittere Angst ist es, die aus Menschen Mumien macht, die leuchtende macht sie zu Dichtern.

Es ist beinah unmöglich, in niemandes Macht zu sein – aber wer das doch zuwege brächte!

Der Schläfer gibt dem Wächter seinen Traum, und dieser hütet ihn, und beide sind zusammen erst ein Raum.

Er bat sie, aus seinen Augen hinauszusteigen.

Er bereitet jedem sein Ende zu und setzt es ihm »Mahlzeit, Mahlzeit!« vor.

Die Schöpfung. »Als es noch Nacht war, war das Licht von einem großen Etwas umschlossen, aus dem es hernach hervorkam. Dieses Etwas hub an, hell zu werden und das Licht, das

V

The responsibility of the mute. A novel.

She says she intends to kill herself, but only after he has apologized to her.

There exists both a luminous and a bitter fear. The first type grows and grows and continues to expand until it bursts. The second type shrinks and shrinks until it dries up. The bitter fear is what turns human beings into mummies; the luminous fear turns them into poets.

It is almost impossible to be in no one's power—but imagine the person who could accomplish that!

The sleeper gives his dream to the guard who watches over it, and it takes both to constitute a space.

He asked her to step out of his eyes.

He prepares an ending for everyone and serves it with the words "Food's here! Come and get it!"

The Creation: "When it was still night, the light was closely wrapped in a great Something, from which it then came forth. This Something became translucent, so as to allow

es in sich barg, zum Vorschein kommen zu lassen. Dann begann es, im Schein des ersten Lichts die Dinge zu erschaffen. Zuerst schuf es große, schwarze Vögel und befahl ihnen in dem Augenblicke, da sie Gestalt angenommen hatten, durch die ganze Welt zu fliegen und aus ihren Schnäbeln einen Hauch ausströmen zu lassen, der reine, strahlende Helle war. Und als die Vögel getan, was ihnen befohlen war, wurde die ganze Welt so hell und licht, wie sie heute ist.«

Chibcha

Das Einzige, was ihn wirklich tröstet, sind Mythen. Sein Herz nährt sich nur von Mythen. Er hebt sich einen Vorrat von unbekannten Mythen auf, sein Lebenselixier. Wenn die Mythen erschöpft sind, muß er sterben.

Das Alter der Erde, meinte er, ändere sich je nach der Zahl ihrer Bewohner.

Am wenigsten verstehe ich mich selbst. Ich will mich gar nicht verstehen. Ich will mich bloß dazu verwenden, um alles zu verstehen, was abgesehen von mir da ist.

In den *platonischen Dialogen*, denen man selbst sozusagen schweigend zuhört, wird man gezwungen, möglichst *langsam* zu begreifen, worum es geht. Manchmal, beinahe widerstrebend, schlägt ein Mythos wie ein Blitz dazwischen ein, aber es wird dafür gesorgt, daß die Atmosphäre gleich danach sich klärt und man nicht mehr zu rasch weiterkommt. Die kraftvolle Entrückung, deren Plato mächtig ist, wird durch den Dialog in einen alltäglichen Gang zurückgeholt, und so erscheint das Großartigste und Unmöglichste plötzlich praktisch.

the light concealed within to make its appearance. Then, in the sheen of this first light, Something began to create all things.

"It first created great black birds, and as soon as they had taken form, It commanded them to fly throughout the whole world and pour from their beaks a breath which was sheer radiant luminosity. And when the birds had performed their task, the whole world became as bright and light-filled as it is today."

Chibcha Indian tale

The only things that truly comfort him are myths. His heart feeds on myths alone. He keeps a reserve of unknown myths as his elixir of life. Once the myths are exhausted he has to die.

He believes that the age of the earth changes according to the size of its population.

I understand myself least of all. I don't even care to understand myself. I only wish to make use of myself, so as to understand everything that exists outside me.

In the Platonic dialogues, to which we listen without saying a word, so to speak, we are forced to comprehend the subject at hand as *slowly* as possible. At times and almost reluctantly, a myth strikes between the lines like a bolt of lightning, but care is taken that the atmosphere is cleared immediately and that we do not progress too rapidly. The rapturous surges of which Plato is capable, are brought back down to earth by the dialogue, and so the most grandiose and impossible notions suddenly appear practical.

Alle Tiere ausgestorben. Werden die Menschen, wenn sie auf keine Tiere mehr sehen, einander immer ähnlicher werden?

Wenn sie ankommen, werfen sie ihre Schuhe zum Fenster hinaus. Dann erfolgt die Begrüßung.

Aus Besorgnis um ihren Charakter hielt sie sich einen Kernbeißer.

Es gibt, glaube ich, kein einziges altes Gebot, das mich nicht in meiner tiefsten Natur beunruhigt und beschäftigt.

Ein Mensch von ungeheuer langem Atem, der sich zu kürzesten Sätzen zwingt.

Geschäfts-Ehen seien die glücklichsten. Dann lieber kein Glück.

Von vielen langjährigen Beziehungen zwischen Menschen bleibt schließlich nichts übrig als ein gegenseitiges *Überwachen*. Alles, worauf man selber Lust hätte, darf der andere nicht tun. Weil man ihn nicht mehr erträgt und darum bestimmt nicht kommt, soll er zu Hause sitzen und auf einen warten. Weil man viel vor ihm verbirgt, soll er keine Geheimnisse haben. Weil man ihn nicht unterhalten mag, soll er unterhaltsam sein.

Er schrieb seine Romane nicht. Er ging sie.

All animals extinct. With no animals to look to, will humans come to resemble one another more and more?

When they arrive, they throw their shoes out the window. Then they proceed to greet each other.

Out of concern for her character, she kept a hawfinch.

I don't think there exists a single ancient commandment which does not touch me in my innermost core and disturb me greatly.

A man with incredibly long breath who forces himself to utter the shortest possible sentences.

It is said that marriages of convenience are the happiest. If that's the case, better do without happiness.

Many long-lasting human relationships ultimately become nothing more than mutual *surveillance*. Everything one person wants to do is forbidden to the other. Because I no longer can stand you and therefore have no intention of joining you, you are to sit at home and wait for me to arrive. Because I keep so much secret from you, you are to have no secrets. Because I do not feel like entertaining you, you are expected to be entertaining.

He didn't write his novels; he walked them.

Er lernt ganze Städte auswendig, bevor er sie sieht. Er liebt die Namen der Straßen, die er noch nicht kennt. Er hat Träume von ihnen, immer sind die Namen lebendiger als die Orte selber.

Die einzigen *vernünftigen* Denker, die er erträgt, sind die Chinesen. Es ist soviel Raum bis zu ihnen hin, sie engen einen nicht ein, wie schön ist die Klugheit, sagt er sich, in der Ferne!

Der Fromme: Gott selbst sei erst am *Entstehen,* er habe die Welt nicht erschaffen, sondern sei ihr Erbe. Im Verlauf der Geschichte, aus manchen ihrer Elemente und Überlieferungen, *bilde* sich Gott. Niemand könne sein Wesen und seine Gestalt vorhersagen, es sei noch zu früh, noch sei es gar nicht gewiß, *wie* Gott sein werde. Einmal werde er sich wahrhaft gebildet haben, und unsere Pflicht sei es, in Ehrfurcht und Erwartung auf diesen Augenblick hin zu leben.

»Ich, keine Religion? Ich habe deren siebzehn, mindestens!« Gérard de Nerval, eines Tages bei Victor Hugo, als man ihn beschuldigte, keine Religion zu haben.

Ein Verdammter in der Hölle, der für jeden Neu-Ankömmling um Gnade bittet.

Du bist aus dem Atem der Welt gerückt, in einen üppigen Kerker, wo kein Wind weht, geschweige denn ein Atem. O weg, weg von allem, das vertraut und persönlich und sicher ist, gib die Vertrautheiten alle auf, sei kühn, wie lange schon schlafen deine hundert Ohren. Sei allein und sag dir die Worte, die niemandem gelten, andere, neue, wie sie der Atem der Welt dir

He learns whole cities by heart before seeing them. He loves the names of the streets he has yet to get to know. He dreams of them, and their names are always more alive than the places themselves.

The only *reasonable* thinkers he can bear are the Chinese. There is so much space between him and them, they don't cramp his style. How beautiful wisdom is—so he tells himself—when it's far away!

The pious man: God Himself is just in the process of *becoming*; He did not create the world but is its heir. God is *being formed* in the course of history, out of some of its elements and traditions. No one can predict God's essence and God's form. It is too early for that, nor is it at all certain *what* God will be like. But one day God truly will have become formed, and it is our duty to live for that moment, in devotion and pious expectation.

"I, no religion? I have seventeen of them, at the very least!" exclaimed Gérard de Nerval when, one day at Victor Hugo's, someone accused him of not having any religion.

One of the damned in hell, who asks forgiveness for any new arrival.

You moved out of the breath of the world and into a luxuriant jail where not a breeze moves, let alone a breath. Oh, away, away from all that which is familiar and personal and secure, renounce all your familiar habits, be daring—for how long have your hundred ears been sleeping? Be alone and say to yourself words not meant for anyone, different words, words such as are bestowed upon you by the breath

gibt. Nimm die bekannten Wege und zerbrich sie überm Knie. Wenn du zu Menschen sprichst, so seien es solche, die du nie wieder siehst. Such den Nabel der Erde. Verachte die Zeit, laß die Zukunft, lumpige Fata Morgana, fahren. Sag nie mehr Himmel. Vergiß, daß es Sterne gab, wirf sie weg wie Krücken. Geh unsicher allein. Schneide keine Sätze mehr aus Papier. Überschwemm dich oder schweige. Schlag die Bäume der Verstellung nieder, es sind nur alte Gebote verkleidet. Ergib dich nicht, der Atem der Welt mag dich wieder fassen und tragen. Du bitte um nichts, und es wird dir nichts gegeben werden. Nackt, wirst du die Schmerzen des Wurmes fühlen, nicht die des Herrn. Spring durch die Lücken der Gnade, tausend Fuß tief. Unten, ganz unten weht der Atem der Welt.

Um das Geringste zu verschweigen, muß sie unendlich viel reden.

Sie fürchtet ihn wie Gott. Er verabscheut sie wie sich selbst.

In jeder einzelnen Beziehung seines Lebens muß er um ein winziges Maß von Gleichgültigkeit kämpfen. Er liebt seine Menschen so sehr, daß er ihre Gedanken rascher bekommt als sie selber. Die Gefahr in ihren Handlungen peinigt ihn, bevor sie noch ahnen, was sie tun werden. Er sieht die Schritte ihrer nächsten Tage und Wochen. Um Monate zu früh stürzt er, für sie. Er haßt sich, für was sie bald tun werden. Ihre Ziele, ihnen noch unbekannt, verfolgen ihn bis in den Traum. Man kann nicht sagen, daß er in seinen Menschen steckt, das wäre zu behaglich. Er *ist* seine Menschen, aber mehr als sie es selber sind.

Das Gedeihen der Welt hängt davon ab, daß man mehr Tiere am Leben erhält. Aber die, die man nicht zu praktischen

of the world. Take your well-known ways and break them over your knee. Speak only to people you will never see again. Seek the navel of the earth. Hold time in disdain, let go of the future, that wretched fata morgana. Never say heaven again. Forget that there were stars, throw them away like crutches. Walk alone, uncertainly. Cut no more sentences out of paper. Inundate yourself or be silent. Chop down those trees of pretense; they are nothing but old commandments in disguise. Do not surrender, for the breath of the world may once again seize and support you. Ask for nothing and nothing will be given you. Naked, you shall feel the pains of the worm, not those of the Lord. Leap through the gaps of mercy, a full thousand feet deep. Down there, all the way down, blows the breath of the world.

So as to conceal even the slightest thing, she has to talk an enormous amount.

She fears him like God. He loathes her as much as he loathes himself.

In every single relation in his life he has to struggle for at least a small measure of indifference. He loves his fellow beings so much that he grasps their thoughts more quickly than they do themselves. Any danger in their actions torments him before they have even an inkling of what they will do. He already foresees what steps they will take during the next days and weeks. Months in advance, he stumbles and falls for them. He hates himself for what they will soon do. Their aims, still unknown to them, haunt his very dreams. It's not that he *lives* in his fellow beings; that sounds too cozy. He *is* his fellow beings, but more so than they are themselves.

Whether the world will prosper will depend on whether more animals will be kept alive. And those animals that are

Zwecken braucht, sind die wichtigsten. Jede Tierart, die stirbt, macht es weniger wahrscheinlich, daß wir leben. Nur angesichts ihrer Gestalten und Stimmen können wir Menschen bleiben. Unsere Verwandlungen nützen sich ab, wenn ihr Ursprung erlischt.

Ich: das *schneidende* Wort.

Nie werde ich das Geheimnis der Worte ergründen, der Sprachen untereinander, und wie die Worte verschiedener Sprachen einander beleben.
Daß ich Gilgamesch sagen kann, Uruk, Engidu und Ischullanu! Hänge ich darum an den Göttern, weil es noch so viele ihrer Namen gibt? Liebe ich die Bibel um der Sprachen willen, in denen sie nun besteht? Sag' ich Pfingsten, weil ich des Zungenredens gedenke? Sind mir die erhabensten Prediger die Kinder der Cevennen?

Die Masse dessen, was sich von einem Menschen erfahren läßt, hat schon als solche Bedeutung und zieht unwiderstehlich an. Man bleibt für alles, was ihn betrifft, erst recht noch weit offen. Es ist nie genug.
Das letzte Beispiel dafür sind die Tagebücher von Thomas Mann, deren Trivialität auf weite Strecken für sie *wirbt*. Es könnte ein weiteres Dutzend Bände davon geben, jeder von ihnen würde begierig gelesen werden.

Es ist beinahe unmöglich, einen Menschen genau so weit zu kennen, daß man ihn immer achten kann. Meist kennt man ihn zu wenig, oft kennt man ihn zu gut. Wer es verstünde, in seiner Kenntnis von Menschen bis an den rechten Punkt vorzudringen und dann stehen zu bleiben, der hätte an ihnen Halt.

not needed for any practical purposes are the most important. Any species of animal which becomes extinct makes it
less likely that we shall survive. We need their forms and
voices to remain human beings. Our own evolution will
cease when its origin is extinguished.

I: the word that *cuts*.

I shall never fathom the secret of words, of languages and
their connections, and how words from different languages
animate each other.
That I am able to say Gilgamesh, Uruk, Enkidu, and Ishu-
lanu! Am I so attached to the gods because so many of their
names still exist? Do I love the Bible for the sake of the
languages of which it is made up? Do I say Pentecost because
it reminds me of talking in tongues? Is this why for me the
children of the Cévennes are the foremost preachers?

The sheer mass that can be learned about someone is in itself
significant and exerts an irresistible attraction. The more one
learns, the more one remains open to any new information
relevant to that person. It is never enough.
The latest illustration of this is Thomas Mann's diaries,
whose long stretches of trivialities actually work in their
favor. There still could be a dozen volumes of them and
each of them would be read avidly.

It is almost impossible to know someone just enough to be
able to respect him at all times. Most often we know him
too little, frequently we know him too well. Whoever could
pursue his knowledge of his fellow men to just the right
depth and then stop, that man would find in them a support
for himself.

Das Glück der Vertriebenen ist das Bessere, dem sie entstammen. Es wird für sie immer besser. Ihr Unglück beginnt, wenn sie dorthin zurückkehren und es so vorfinden, wie sie es verloren haben, um allen Glanz der Erinnerung betrogen.

Durch nichts, was er unterdrückt, kann der Mensch besser werden. Der einzige Weg zur Änderung geht durch die Verwandlungen, die man für seine Schlechtigkeiten findet. Aber diese Verwandlungen müssen stimmen und überraschen, sonst reizen sie zu neuen Schlechtigkeiten. Meist springt eine von diesen für die andere ein, und das Spiel geht unkenntlich und vergnüglich weiter.

Freunde sind Leute, denen man großartige Nachrichten über sich vorsetzt, und es macht nichts, daß sie nie wahr werden.

Einer, den man nur kennt, wenn es Tag wird.

Den Himmel *betasten*.

Ein Tiger, der kein Blut mehr sehen kann.

Solange es den Tod gibt, ist Demut nicht möglich.

Worauf er aus ist? Auf *Meistdeutigkeit*.

Ein Gott, so winzig, daß er in jedes Geschöpf hineinschlüpft.

The good fortune of exiles consists in their loss of Something Better at their origin. But then their life gets better all the time. Their misfortune begins when they return to where they came from and find everything as they lost it, stripped of the dazzle of memory.

Man cannot improve himself by anything that he suppresses. The only path to change leads through the transformations he discovers for his evil traits. But these transformations must work, they must surprise, or else they merely will provoke new evil. In most cases, one bad trait merely supplants another, and so the game continues merrily along, undetected.

Friends are people whom one presents with splendid accounts of oneself, and it doesn't matter that these accounts never come true.

A man one knows only at daybreak.

To touch the skies.

A tiger who no longer can stand the sight of blood.

For as long as death exists, humility is not possible.

What is he after? Ambiguity? No, *multiguity*.

A god so minuscule he can slip into any creature.

Alle Geschichtsschreibung, die nicht von Namen prall ist, langweilt dich. Es ist nämlich dieselbe Geschichte, und das Neue sind nur die Namen. Aber durch die Namen ist auch die Geschichte immer neu. Sie sind es, die die Geschichte auf eine mysteriöse Weise verändern, und man wäre versucht sich zu fragen, ob sie sich nicht vielleicht nur innerhalb von Namen abspielt.

Einer, der sein ganzes Leben nie ein schlechtes Wort über jemanden gesagt hat. Wie muß er sich selber zugerichtet haben!

Andere mögen ihren Schutzengel haben, er hat einen *Schutzvogel*.

»Seid sparsam. Singet nicht im Leben und trauert nicht im Tod.« (Mo-Tse) Auch das ist Chinesisch. Was ist nicht Chinesisch?

Das Verhaltene der Stirn, als ob dahinter die Geschichte aller Menschen schliefe.

Eine *Farbe*, die einen Menschen vernichtet.

Hätte er die Zeit genützt, es wäre nichts aus ihm geworden.

Die chinesische Geschichte wimmelt von *fetten* Rebellen.

Immer wenn ihn die Adjektive überfallen, wird er lächerlich. Sie enthalten seine Gefühle.

All historiography not chock-full of names bores you. For indeed the story is always the same and only the names are new. But because of the names, the history, too, is always new. It is they which in a mysterious way change history, and we are tempted to wonder whether in truth history does not take place merely within names.

Someone who during his entire life never said one bad word about someone else. How badly he must have dealt with himself!

Others may have their guardian angel; he has a *guardian bird*.

"Be thrifty. Do not sing in life and do not mourn in death." (*Mo-tze*) Even this is Chinese. What isn't?

The stubborn reticence of the forehead, as if the history of all mankind slept behind it.

A *color* which destroys a man.

If he had made good use of his time, he never would have amounted to anything.

Chinese history is brimming with *fat* rebels.

Whenever he is assaulted by adjectives, he becomes ridiculous. They contain his emotions.

Wie verächtlich ist der Mensch, wenn er vor nichts mehr
Angst hat! Das Kern-Dilemma jeder Utopie. Unsäglich
schmal der Weg zwischen zu viel und zu wenig Angst.

Die Kraft des Entdeckens gibt ihm sein größtes Selbstgefühl.
Was für andere der Kampf ist, ist für ihn die Entdeckung.
Aber es ist möglich, daß er alles, was er zu entdecken glaubt,
erfindet und als ein Mensch von heute die Illusion der Entdek-
kung dafür beansprucht.

Die Geschichte des Feldzugs Napoleons in Rußland gelesen,
in Chateaubriands ›Mémoires d'Outre-Tombe‹.
Peinliches Gefühl. Chateaubriand war selbst nicht dort. Es
ist, als reklamiere er die Opfer für sich.

Das Unglück der Moral: daß sie alles besser weiß und darum
nichts *erfährt*.

Wenn er sehr verzweifelt ist, muß er jemanden trösten und ist
plötzlich selber getröstet.

Lesen, während die Uhr vernehmlich tickt – verantwortliches
Lesen.
Lesen während alle Uhren stehen, glückliches Lesen.

›Eraritjaritjaka‹ – ein archaischer poetischer Ausdruck auf Ar-
anda, bedeutet »voller Verlangen nach etwas was verloren gegangen ist«.

How despicable is a person who no longer fears anything! The central dilemma of any utopia. How ineffably narrow the path running between too much fear and too little!

The power of discovery bestows upon him his fullest sense of self. What struggle is for others, the experience of discovery is for him. Though it is possible that he is really inventing what he believes he has discovered and, being a man of our time, is merely claiming the illusion of discovery.

Have read the history of Napoleon's campaign in Russia in Chateaubriand's *Mémoires d'Outre-tombe*.
A feeling of embarrassment. Chateaubriand was not there in person. It is as if he were claiming the victims for himself.

The misfortune of ethics: because it knows everything better, it *learns* nothing.

Whenever he is in great despair, he need only comfort someone else—and all of a sudden feels comforted himself.

To read while the clock is audibly ticking: responsible reading. To read while all clocks have stopped: happy reading.

"Erarityarityake"—an archaic poetic expression in the Arunta language meaning "full of desire for something that has been lost."

Prophezeiungen, die eingetroffen sind, mißtraut er am meisten.

Dieser peinliche Zwang, überall und in allen Mythen *ein- und denselben* zu sehen: nichts scheint sinnloser, nichts stößt mich mehr ab. Denn die Unterschiedlichkeit der Mythen, und sie allein, ist unser rasch schwindender Reichtum und unsere Hoffnung.

Du hast so viel gegen die großen Männer auf dem Herzen. – Gefallen dir die Kleinen besser? – Manche.

Ich möchte so alt werden, daß der Gedanke an alles, was ich nicht erfahren habe, mich nicht mehr peinigt.

»Die Ewe in Togo halten sich Meerkatzen, die so gezähmt und gelehrig sind, daß man sie als Verkäufer verwendet; man hängt ihnen eine Kürbisschale um den Hals, die Bündel von Tabakblättern zu je 5 Pfennigen enthält, und schickt sie damit auf den Markt. Nimmt ein Käufer ein Bündel heraus, ohne das entsprechende Geldstück in die Schale zu legen, *so folgt der Affe ihm so lange, bis er bezahlt hat.*«
Diedrich Westermann, Die Kpelle

Den Sinn *verhalten*, nichts ist so widernatürlich wie die unaufhörliche Aufdeckung des Sinns. Der Vorzug und die eigentliche Macht der Mythen: daß der Sinn nicht genannt wird.

Gottes Trotz: er muß den Menschen entfernen.

He most distrusts those prophecies which have been fulfilled.

This irksome compulsion to see in all myths *one and the same*: nothing seems more senseless, nothing revolts me more. For it is precisely the variety—and that alone!—among the myths which constitutes our rapidly dwindling wealth and our remaining hope.

You have so much against great men. — Do you like the little ones better? — Some.

I would like to grow old enough so that the thought of everything I failed to experience would no longer torment me.

"The Ewe people of Togo keep long-tailed monkeys as pets which are so tame and teachable they are used as salespersons; the Ewes hang an empty gourd around their necks containing bundles of tobacco leaves selling for five cents each and send the monkeys, thus equipped, to market. If a buyer takes a tobacco bundle from the gourd without dropping in the appropriate coin, *the monkey will follow him around until he has paid up.*"

Diedrich Westermann, The Chapel

To *withhold* meaning: nothing is quite so unnatural as the constant uncovering of meanings. The merit and the true power of the myth: its meaning remains concealed.

God's defiance: He has to keep Man at a distance.

Empfindlichkeit, die keinen Spott erlaubt. *Rousseau* als das Anti-Lukianische in der Literatur. Rousseau beißt nicht. Seine Sätze dienen nicht als Werkzeug der Zerkleinerung. Alles ist auf Verbesserung hin angelegt, aus Krankheit strebt alles nach Gesundheit. Das Gute ist nicht unbekannt, es war schon da und muß wiederhergestellt werden. Das Gute hat eine unerschütterliche Meinung von sich und mißtraut Mächtigen, die es auch verachtet. In Voltaire gerät Rousseau an das Lukianische, das im französischen Wesen des 18. Jahrhunderts zu einer Art von absoluter Macht gelangt ist. Nach Rousseau wird – sobald die anderen erkennen, daß das Gute seine höchste und selbstverständliche Instanz ist – unaufhörlich geschnappt, er ist – daran ist nicht zu zweifeln – von einer Meute von Feinden umringt, und sein Verfolgungsgefühl ist berechtigt. Daß er nicht immer genau erkennt, von wem der letzte Feindschaftsakt ausgeht, ist nicht zu verwundern. Es sind ihrer zu viele, sie folgen sich zu rasch, instinktiv tut er das Richtige, um sich seiner Paranoia zu erwehren: er wechselt häufig den Standort.

In seiner Verwirrung wird der Mensch, der daran war, alles zu vernichten, wieder ergreifend.
Vielleicht gibt er's im letzten Augenblick auf.
Für wie lange?

Es gibt Sätze in der Bibel, die auf Umwegen und von jeder Frömmigkeit entbunden, zu einem wiederkehren. Einer, der in solchen Sätzen besonders erfahren war und es wußte, war Goethe.

VI

A sensitivity intolerant of all derision. Rousseau, the anti-Lucian, the anti-satirical principle in literature: Rousseau does not bite. His sentences do not serve as tools for belittlement. Everything is directed toward improvement; from affliction, everything strives toward health. Goodness is not unknown, it has been here before and merely needs to be re-established. Goodness has an unshakably high opinion of itself and distrusts the powerful, whom it also despises. In Voltaire, Rousseau encountered the principles of Lucian which had come to dominate the thinking of eighteenth-century France. As soon as Rousseau's contemporaries realized that he considered goodness the highest authority—and a self-evident one—they started snarling at him, and there can be no doubt that he was surrounded by a pack of enemies, so that his feeling of persecution was indeed justified. It is not surprising that he occasionally failed to recognize exactly who was responsible for the latest act of animosity. He had too many enemies, they followed one another in too rapid succession, and so to ward off his paranoia, he instinctively did the right thing: he frequently changed his position.

On the verge of destroying everything, Man, in his very confusion, becomes touching once more.
Perhaps he'll give it up at the last moment.
But for how long?

There are sentences in the Bible which, stripped of all piousness, come back to us in roundabout ways. Goethe was particularly well versed in such sentences—and he knew it, too.

Er verscherzt sich alle Freunde, indem er sich des Anspruchs entkleidet.

Laß ihn nur rauschen, er klatscht sich Beifall.

Es ist an Tieren etwas, das ihn besänftigt, an allen nämlich, die ihn zum Verstummen reizen.

Er horcht im Weltraum auf letzte Gedanken.

Vernichtungs-Schwätzer, und in der Sprache, in der es das Wort ›Vernichtung‹ gibt.

Rückkehr zu Sophokles:
Die Mädchen von Trachis
Jole, der eigentliche Gegenstand des Unglücks von Herakles und Dejaneira, ist stumm. Sie erscheint, sie fällt Dejaneira auf, doch sie spricht nie ein Wort. Sie schwindet ins Haus und erscheint nie wieder. Diese in Worten ausgesparte Figur ist, was mich an diesem Stück wirklich bewegt. Alles geschieht um sie. Sie hat erst keinen Namen, er wird verleugnet. Dejaneira fühlt sich von ihr angezogen; doch dann stellt sich heraus, daß ihr Name wie ihre Geschichte am Marktplatz öffentlich ausgerufen worden sind und nur von Dejaneira geheimgehalten wurden.
Herakles liebt sie so, daß es inmitten seiner Brände zu seinem letzten Wunsch wird, Hyllos, sein Sohn, möge sie heiraten.

He forfeits all his friends by divesting himself of any claims on them.

Let him go on roaring—he is merely applauding himself.

There is something in animals which soothes him, at least in the ones that leave him speechless with awe.

He hearkens in cosmic space to ultimate thoughts.

People who babble about annihilation, and in a language which contains the word "annihilation."

Back to Sophocles.
The Maids of Trachis
Iole, the true focus of the tragedy of Herakles and Deianeira, is mute. She appears, she draws the attention of Deianeira, but she never utters a single word. She disappears into the house and never again reemerges. It is this figure, bereft of words, which truly moves me in this play. Everything revolves around her. At first, she has no name; her name is denied her. Deianeira feels attracted to her: but then it turns out that Iole's name and story had already been proclaimed in the marketplace; only Deianeira was not in on the secret.
Herakles loves her so much that, even as he is consumed by flames, his last wish is that his son Hyllos marry her.

Philoktetes
Spiel der Verstellung. Entwandlung zur Wahrheit: Neoptole-
mos. Felseninsel, der einsame Philoktet. Seine Schmerzen.
Sein Anfall. Danach der Schlaf. Sein Wert ist sein Bogen, von
Herakles hinterlassen, zum Dank für den Feuertod aus eben-
solchen Giftschmerzen.
Ein frauenloses Stück. Keine Frau wird darin erwähnt. Die
Feigheit des Odysseus: er flieht vor der Drohung des Bogens,
den Neoptolemos hält.
Merkwürdig *einsam* das Stück über Philoktet. Keine Masse
nah dahinter, die Kämpfenden um Troja weit überm Meer. Es
spielt alles in der Nähe der Doppelhöhle.
Das Leiden des Philoktet über zehn Jahre hinausgezogen, immer erneuert, durch Schlaf nach jedem Anfall unterbrochen.
(Im Gegensatz zum raschen, verzehrenden Schmerz des Herakles.)
Der *Starrsinn* des Philoktet ist ein Starrsinn durch Schmerz.
Die Gewöhnung an ihn, an seine Stätte, ist wirksamer als die
ans Alter.
Der Schluß, das Erscheinen des Herakles (immerhin der eigentliche Inhaber des Bogens, auf den alles ankommt), wie bei Euripides, für unsereins schwer akzeptabel, opernhafte Lösung zu
aller Gunsten.

Elektra
Erste Erkennung am Grab, wo die jüngere Schwester Chrisothymis Haar von Orest findet. Doch glaubt ihr Elektra nicht,
unter dem Eindruck des furchtbaren Berichts vom Wagenrennen, bei dem Orest verunglückt sei. Elektra ist in Verzweiflung
und seines Todes gewiß, und dann ist er da und gibt sich zu erkennen: Rückkehr des Toten.
Die Erkennungsszene ist aufs höchste gesteigert, durch die
Urne mit seiner vermeintlichen Asche, die unerkannt Orest in
Händen hält. Elektra will diese Asche, Orest verteidigt sie
schwach, im Kampf um sie bricht sein Widerstand zusammen,
und er gibt sich zu erkennen.

Philoctetes

A play of dissimulation. Transmutations toward truth: Neoptolemos. A rocky island, the solitary Philoctetes. His sufferings. His seizure. Followed by sleep. His treasure is the bow he received from Hercules in gratitude for the fiery death by which Philoctetes released the hero from the painful fire of poison.

A play without women. No woman is ever mentioned in it. The cowardice of Odysseus: he flees when threatened by the bow held by Neoptolemos.

A strangely *solitary* play, this play of Philoctetes' fate. No crowds close behind, the warriors fighting for Troy far away beyond the sea. Everything happens near the twin caves.

The sufferings of Philoctetes drawn out over ten years, always renewed, interrupted by sleep after each seizure. (In contrast to the rapidly consuming suffering of Herakles.)

The *obstinacy* of Philoctetes is an obstinacy derived from pain. Becoming accustomed to pain and to its location is more effective than becoming accustomed to old age.

The conclusion, the apparition of Herakles (the true owner, after all, of the bow on which all depends), just as in Euripides and rather difficult for us to accept, an operatic solution, for the good of all.

Electra

First recognition at the grave, where the younger sister Chrisothymis finds some hair belonging to Orestes. But Electra does not believe her: she is still stricken by the terrible news of the chariot race in which Orestes allegedly had his fatal accident. Electra is in despair, she is convinced he is dead. Then suddenly he appears and reveals his identity: a return from the dead.

The scene of recognition is heightened to the utmost by the urn supposedly containing his ashes, which Orestes, still unrecognized, is holding in his hands. Electra wants those ashes, Orestes weakly wards her off, and in this struggle his resistance collapses and he reveals his true identity.

Diese Erkenntnis dessen, der ›seine eigene‹ Asche in der Hand hält, ist dramatisch ein großer Einfall, doch hat er etwas Frevelhaftes: der Frevel des Dichters, der der Konsequenz seines Einfalls alles zu opfern bereit ist.

Alle Beziehungen zum Tod enthält ›Elektra‹, sogar diese, die der Rückkehr.

Der Zusammenstoß mit Klytämnestra ist schonungslos, von ungeheurer Kraft. Die mörderische Mutter, von einem Traum beunruhigt, will am Grab des Ermordeten opfern, es ist dasselbe Grab, an dem der Rächer, der Sohn, soeben erschienen war, um sich Kraft zur Rache zu holen.

Ganz urtümlich das Recht auf Rache. Mord und Tod sind getrennt, verpönt das eine, das andere als Lebensinhalt des Kriegers und Helden gebilligt.

Elektra lebt wie ein Bettelweib im Haus ihres ermordeten Vaters. Seit zehn Jahren hat sie keinen anderen Gedanken als den der Rache. In Jahren gesteigerte Affekte sind ein dramatisches Anliegen des Sophokles (der Schmerz des Philoktet, Ödipus der Blinde).

Elektra wartet zehn Jahre auf das Heranwachsen des Bruders, den sie gerettet hat. In Angst vor seiner Rache leben Klytämnestra und Ägisth.

Es ist der älteste Tod, ungebrochen in all seinen Traditionen, von dem dieses Drama erfüllt ist. Drum ist auch die Szene zwischen Mörderin und Rächerin unentbehrlich.

Elektras Lähmung durch die Nachricht vom Tode ihres Bruders steht für alle Nachrichten vom Tode Nächster. Ihre Wirkung ist gesteigert durch das zehnjährige Warten auf ihn. Elektra, vernichtet, nimmt das Amt der Rache auf sich, es gibt keinen Bruder mehr, dem es zukäme.

Die Figur der Elektra ist darum überwältigend, weil sich nichts in ihr ändert und nie etwas ändern wird.

Dieser eine bestimmte Tod, der Mord am Vater, ist immer da, in Gefühl und Gedanken, durch nichts zu beruhigen, durch nichts abzulenken. Wenn es auch, für uns heute lästig, um Rache geht, so bleibt es doch Rache um *diesen* Tod, mit keinem

This recognition of someone who is holding "his own ashes" is a great dramatic inspiration, but there is something sacrilegious about it: the sacrilege of the poet prepared to sacrifice everything to the logic of his inspiration.

Electra contains all possible relationships with death, even the return from death. The collision with Clytemnestra is brutal and full of enormous power. The murderous mother, troubled by a dream, is driven to make a sacrificial offering at the grave of the man she had murdered, the same grave at which the avenger, her own son, had appeared a moment earlier to gather strength for the act of revenge.

This right to revenge as something entirely primordial. Murder and killing are separate, one a strict taboo, the other an approved way of life for warrior and hero.

Electra lives like a beggar in the house of her murdered father. For ten years she thinks of nothing but revenge. Passions intensified by years are a primary dramatic concern to Sophocles (the suffering Philoctetes; the blinded Oedipus). Electra waits for ten years for the brother she saved to come of age. Clytemnestra and Aegisthus live in fear of his avenging wrath. The tragedy is filled with this oldest kind of killing, unbroken in any of its traditions. And this is why the scene between the murderess and the avenging Electra is indispensable.

Electra's paralysis, brought on by the news of her brother's death, stands for the effect produced by all reports concerning the deaths of our nearest and dearest. Here the effect is intensified by the ten years of waiting for the allegedly deceased brother. A shattered Electra takes upon herself the task of revenge, since there is no longer a brother to whom this task would, by right, belong.

The figure of Electra is overwhelming because nothing ever changes and nothing ever will change inside her.

The one specific death, the murder of the father, is always present in her thoughts and emotions, nothing can assuage her, nothing can distract her. Even though the core of the play is revenge—for us a somewhat uncomfortable theme —it is nevertheless this *one single* death, not to be confused

anderen zu verwechseln. Nie wird er hingenommen, nie wird der Schmerz um ihn sich beruhigen. Die Treue zum Toten ist die eigentliche Treue, es gibt keine Treue, die sich mit dieser vergleichen läßt. Die Götter haben damit wenig, nur ›pro forma‹ zu tun. Alles spielt sich in Elektra selbst ab. Sie ist stark und unablenkbar, aber sie ist es durch diesen Tod und wäre durch nichts anderes je so geworden. Es ist ein früher Tod, und es ist ein Mord. –

Zwischen beiden Schwestern steht die Frage der Macht. Ob der Machtlose sich ihr fügt, ob nicht. Für Elektra stellt sich diese Frage nicht, denn die Macht, der man sich zu fügen hätte, wäre eben die der Mörder.

Elektra steht draußen, während ihre Mutter innen im Hause von Orest erschlagen wird. Es ist, als führte Elektra selbst die Schläge. Ägisth muß Orest vorangehen, an die Stätte seiner eigenen Tat an Agamemnon. An dieser selben Stätte wird er erschlagen. Dann bricht alles ab, mit drei Zeilen, einem einzigen Satz. (1986)

Ödipus auf Kolonos

Es bewegt mich mehr als jedes der anderen Dramen, vielleicht weil Ödipus sein Grab selbst bestimmt. Der Fluch am Sohn Polyneikes. Das zärtliche Gespräch zwischen Antigone und dem Bruder, *nachdem* dieser vom Vater verflucht ist.

Es wäre in allen griechischen Dramen die Stelle des *Grabes* zu bestimmen.

Im Ödipus auf Kolonos ist es segenstiftend, aber nicht genau bezeichnet. Zeuge des Todes und Grabes ist Theseus allein.

Der Schutz, den er gewährt, ist wie der eines Gottes. Dieser zweite Ödipus ist im Augenblick des Untergangs von Athen geschrieben, eine Verherrlichung der Stadt in ihrer schwersten Zeit, von Sophokles, der die Jahre ihres Glanzes gekannt hat, der mit Perikles befreundet war und mit ihm zusammen gekämpft hat.

with any other. This death will never be accepted and the pain it caused will never be assuaged. Fidelity to the dead father is the one true fidelity; no other can compare with it. The gods have little to do with it, a mere pro forma connection. Everything takes place within Electra herself. She is strong and unwavering in her purpose, but she is so only by reason of her father's death; nothing else ever could have shaped her thus. It is a premature death and, moreover, it is murder.

The two sisters are divided by the question of whether someone who is powerless will or will not submit to power. This question does not arise for Electra, for the power to which she would have to submit would be that of the murderer. Electra stands outside while, inside the house, her mother is slain by Orestes. Yet it is as if Electra herself were striking the blows. Aegisthus must precede Orestes to the site of his own attack on Agamemnon. He is slain at the same site. Then everything breaks off, in three lines, a single sentence.

(1986)

Oedipus at Colonus

This one moves me more than all the other tragedies, perhaps because Oedipus himself determines the site of his grave. His cursing of his son Polynices. The loving conversation between Antigone and her brother, after the latter had been cursed by his father.

In every Greek tragedy, the *grave site* should be located.

In *Oedipus at Colonus*, the grave site is benevolent and beneficial, but its location is obscure. Only Theseus is witness to both the death and the grave.

The protection Theseus grants resembles that of a god. This second *Oedipus* was written during the decline of Athens as a glorification of the city in its darkest hour, by Sophocles, who had known its years of greatest glory, who had been the friend of Pericles and who had fought alongside him.

Unter dem Eindruck der Pest entstand der erste Ödipus, unter der Drohung des Untergangs der zweite.

Im ›Kolonos‹ hat Ödipus Begegnungen mit Fremden oder Feinden. Theseus der Einzige ist ihm gut gesinnt und mächtig wie ein Gott. Die anderen kommen ihn holen, um sich seiner Leiche und seines Grabes zu versichern. Er reißt Kreon die falsche Maske vom Gesicht und verflucht seinen Sohn Polyneikes. Dieser weiß nun, nach dem Fluch des Vaters, daß der Kampf, in den er auszieht, verloren ist. Er zieht wissend, trotz der flehentlichen Bitte seiner Schwester Antigone, in den verlorenen Krieg. Er kann nicht zurück, es ist die Erfahrung vieler Athener in *ihrem* Krieg, die ihn doch weiter kämpften.

Die griechische Tragödie, die keine Ablenkung erlaubt. Der Tod – des einzelnen – hat noch sein volles Gewicht. Mord, Selbstmord, Begräbnis und Grabstätte, es ist alles exemplarisch da, nackt und unverschönt; auch die Klage (bei uns kastriert); auch der Schmerz der Schuldigen.

Wahrhaftig verändert hat sich in unserer Zeit die Mitwelt des Todes. Seine Massenhaftigkeit ist nicht mehr die Ausnahme, alles mündet in sie. In der Beschleunigung zu ihr hin verliert der Einzeltod an Gewicht. So viel mehr Menschen – sollen sie noch einzeln sterben? Wenn sie es nicht mehr dürfen, wird der Punkt erreicht sein, von dem es keine Rückkehr mehr gibt.

Er braucht chinesische Unsterbliche, zur Korrektur der unseren.

Was beim Volke Shakespeares heute als ›gloom‹ gilt.

Er nahm kein Buch zu sich, ohne es auf die Stirn zu küssen.

The first *Oedipus* was written under the impact of the plague, the second one under the threat of annihilation.

In *Colonus*, Oedipus encounters only strangers and enemies. Theseus, powerful as a god, is the only one who is well disposed toward him. The others come to fetch him so as to secure his remains and his grave. He tears off the false mask of Creon and curses his son Polynices, who now realizes that the battle he is in is already lost. In spite of all his sister Antigone's imploring, he sets out to fight a losing war. He cannot turn back, and this is the fate of many Athenians in *their* war, which they nevertheless persisted in fighting.

Greek tragedy does not allow for any distraction. Death— of the individual—still has its full weight. Murder, suicide, funeral, and grave site, everything is there in exemplary simplicity, naked and unadorned; even the lament (castrated in our times); even the pain of the guilty.

What has changed radically in our times is the ever-present world of death. Its appearance as a mass phenomenon is no longer exceptional; everything flows into it. Hurtling toward this vast sea of death, the individual death loses its weight. There are so many more people now—are they all expected to die singly? When they are no longer allowed to do so, we shall have reached the point of no return.

Chinese immortals are needed to correct our own.

The meaning of "gloom" in Shakespeare's nation today.

He never picks up a book without kissing it on the forehead.

Arthur Waley: Der Hochmut des englischen Kastensystems war zum Hochmut seiner Gelehrsamkeit geworden. Er gab vor, diese für selbstverständlich zu halten, als wäre sie etwas Angeborenes. Leute, mit denen er umging, sollten ihn verstehen, selbst das Entlegenste teilte er ihnen ohne Vorbereitung mit. Plötzlich war es gesagt. Doch dann verstummte er und verharrte in seinem beleidigenden Schweigen. Was hatte er einem nicht zugetraut! Und wie war man plötzlich Luft für ihn! Aller Hochmut, unter dem er gelitten hatte, wurde von ihm so auf unschuldige Weise abgegolten. Er gehörte nicht wirklich zur Bloomsbury Group, obwohl er mitten unter den ihr Angehörigen wohnte. Aufgenommen wurde er von den Sitwells, die man als eine plakative Essenz des Englischen bezeichnen könnte. Diese nannte er, besonders oft aber Edith Sitwell, es war beinahe so, wie man höher gestellte Mitglieder seiner eigenen Familie nennt. Diese gewährten ihm auch die Bewunderung, die er verdiente.

Von eigenen Urteilen war er erfüllt und äußerte sie schneidend, unerträglich wäre es ihm gewesen, dasselbe wie andere zu denken. Die Weltliteratur, nicht nur die des Ostens, war ihm in einem Maße vertraut wie niemand sonst, den ich in England kannte. Durch ihn ist vieles aus China und Japan in sie eingegangen, und was vor ihm für den Westen nur dem Namen nach bestand, ist heute für jeden zugänglich.

Er ist 77 Jahre alt geworden und war nie in China.

Ein Garten, welch ein Garten, den man nie an der gleichen Stelle betritt!

Im Alter *kommentiert* man die großen Bücher. Es sind dieselben, die man jung in Stücke zu reißen suchte. Da es nicht gelang, versuchte man's wieder. Man ließ sie liegen. Man vergaß sie. Nun sind sie wieder da. Durch die Jahre des Vergessens hat man sie sich verdient. Man betrachtet ihre Herrlich-

Arthur Waley: The arrogance of the British caste system became the arrogance of his erudition. He pretended it was something a person is innately given. The people he consorted with were expected to understand him; he would impart to them the most arcane bit of knowledge without any preparation. He would utter it all of a sudden, and then fall silent just as abruptly and remain in this insulting silence. The things he expected us to understand! And how quickly we would cease to exist for him! In this way, he unwittingly compensated for all the arrogance he himself had been made to suffer. He didn't really belong to the Bloomsbury circle, even though he lived right in the middle of it. He had been taken up by the Sitwells, who could be defined as a cartoonish essence of Britishness. He often referred to them, particularly to Edith Sitwell, the way one refers to higher-placed members of one's own family. They, in turn, granted him the admiration he indeed deserved.

He was full of his own opinions, which he would voice in a cutting way; it would have been quite intolerable to him to think the same thoughts as others. World literature, not merely that of the East, was more familiar to him than to anyone else I knew in England. He added much to it from China and Japan, which earlier in the West was known by name only, but which, thanks to him, is now accessible to anyone.

He lived to be seventy-seven and never set foot in China.

A garden, but what a garden: one which is never entered at the same place!

In old age we write *commentaries* on the great books, the same ones we sought to tear to pieces when we were young. Having failed in this, we tried again. Then we let them lie. We forgot them. But now they are back. And now we deserve them by virtue of having forgotten them for so many

keiten. Man spricht zu ihnen. Jetzt, denkt man, müßte man
ein neues Leben beginnen, um ein einziges von ihnen zu verstehen.

Ein Geist, der an seinem Vergessenen von Zeit zu Zeit wieder
aufblüht.
Dauerblütler wie Schopenhauer: bei ihnen war *nichts* vergessen.

Wäre Timon nicht reich gewesen – was wäre Timon?
Er wäre nichts, wenn er es noch wäre.

»Es zeigt von schwachem Verstand, wenn ein Mann viele
Freunde hat.« *Darani*

»Der Gerechte verändert sich vierzigmal am Tage, aber der
Heuchler verbleibt vierzig Jahre lang in demselben Zustand.«

Dummkopf beim Rennen. Wie schön sind Beine allein.

Menschen, die an der Sonne schlecht und gehässig werden.
Menschen, denen Kälte und Finsternis gut tun.

Er spricht nur zu Nützlichkeiten.

Wieviele hat Nietzsche mit Lust auf Gefahren erfüllt! Dann
waren die Gefahren da, und sie gingen *kläglich* unter.

years. Now we behold their splendor. We speak to them.
We think that now would be the time to begin a new life,
just in order to truly understand even a single one of them.

A spirit who from time to time blossoms out from the
forgotten.
Constant bloomers such as Schopenhauer: those who forgot
nothing.

If Timon had not been wealthy—what would Timon be?
He would be nothing—if he still were at all.

"The possession of many friends is proof of a weak mind."
                                                            Darani

"The just man changes forty times a day but the hypocrite
remains the same for forty years."

An idiot at a footrace: how beautiful all those legs are by
themselves!

People in whom the sun brings out evil and spite.
People who thrive in darkness and cold.

He only speaks to useful things.

How many people Nietzsche inspired with a craving for
danger! Then the dangers materialized and they all failed
miserably.

Vielleicht die reinste Genugtuung meines Lebens: Musils Geltung.

Einer, den Namen *schmerzen*, nicht nur die der Zeitgenossen.

Die Verachtung für einen, der nichts will, oder nicht will, was alle unaufhörlich wollen.

»Nobody running at full speed has either a head or a heart.«
Yeats

»Das Leben ist nichts Wichtiges. Alle deine Sklaven leben, alle Tiere.«
Seneca, erbärmlich!

Unter früheren Daten eintragen, als ließe sich das Vergangene beeinflussen.

Er nimmt nichts zurück. Sein Stolz auf dieses Nichts.

Perhaps the purest satisfaction of my life: the renown gained by Musil.

Someone to whom *names* cause pain, and not merely those of his contemporaries.

The contempt for someone who does not want anything, or who does not want what everyone else constantly desires.

"Nobody running at full speed has either a head or a heart."
Yeats

"Life is not important. All of your slaves are alive, and so are all the animals."
Seneca—despicable!

To predate entries: as if the past could be altered!

He retracts nothing. What pride he takes in precisely this nothing.

VII

»Das Leben ist so köstlich, daß ich es nicht wagen würde, mir
etwas Schöneres auszumalen als das Leben.«

Jules Renard

Er saß da und sprach. Einige Stunden saß er da und sprach von
seiner Glorie. Es ging ihm um nichts dahinter, die Glorie war
sich genug, sein Name war einer, den hunderttausend tragen.

Zum Entstellen zieht er die Kleider des Preisens an.

Haustiere wichtiger als Geld.
»Für zehn Prozent der befragten Engländer waren die Haustiere wichtiger für das persönliche Glück als der Ehepartner.
Zwanzig Prozent der Befragten fanden Haustiere wichtiger
als Kinder und mehr als ein Drittel der Befragten hielten
ihre Haustiere für wichtiger als ihre Arbeit. *Fast die Hälfte
aller Interviewten fanden Haustiere wichtiger als Geld*, und
94 Prozent beschäftigten sich lieber mit ihren Tieren als vor
dem Fernseher zu sitzen!«

›Sentimental‹, welch ein Wort! Ich *habe* Gefühle und werde
mich ihrer nicht schämen. Ich will sie nicht unterdrücken, ich
will sie haben. Es sind sehr viele, sie widersprechen einander,
man soll nicht versuchen, sie zu einer Mittellinie zu reduzie-
ren. Wenn sie zu heftig ausschlagen, darf man sie zur Beruhi-
gung verzeichnen.
Aber es ist wahr, daß Rousseau z. B. mir eben durch seine Sen-
timentalität oft unerträglich war. Das hängt damit zusammen,

VII

"Life is so delightful that I wouldn't dare try imagining anything finer."

Jules Renard

He sat there and spoke. For hours on end he sat there and spoke of his glory. He had no ulterior motive, the glory was sufficient in itself; hundreds of thousands bear his name.

For the act of defacement he assumes the clothing of eulogy.

Pets more important than money:
"For ten percent of Englishmen polled, pets were more important to their personal happiness than spouses. Twenty percent of those polled considered pets more important than children and more than a third of these valued their pets more than their work. *Almost half of those interviewed thought their pets more important than money,* and 94 percent preferred spending time with their pets to watching TV!"

"Sentimental": what a word! I *do* have feelings and I will not be ashamed of them. I do not wish to suppress them: I *want* them. There are a great many of them, they contradict each other, they should not be reduced to a tepid median. If they lash out too violently, they may be calmed by being recorded.
However, it is true that I often found Rousseau, for instance, unbearable because of his sentimentality. That has to do with

daß man den Mann, der seine vielen Gefühle vorführt, nicht wirklich mag. Sie sind zu körperlich und geben sich zu gern als selbstlos.

Denkt man aber an seine gefühlsmäßige Wirkung auf andere, so scheint er unermeßlich, und es wird beinahe gleichgültig, wie die Wirkung seiner Gefühle auf ihn selber war.

Es gibt *schlichte* Eigenschaften an Menschen, für die man seine Seele verkaufen könnte.

Wie schön er wird im Bereuen! Wem hilft es? Dem Zuschauer.

Er kommt sich vor wie ein Dieb an der Welt. Mehr und mehr Wunderbares wird er nie kennenlernen.

Entwertung durch Wiederholung. Erregung durch Wiederholung?

Das größte Erlebnis nach Büchner war William Blake, in England.
Das früheste Erlebnis als Kind war Swift, ebendort.
England liegt für mich zwischen Swift und Blake.

Es kommen keine neuen Orte bei dir hinzu. Aber wie sich die alten *stärken*! Sie graben sich förmlich in die Erde ein und schicken nach dir, sie ziehen dich hin, sie rufen, sie schreien, und es ist sehr wahrscheinlich, daß sie dich spät noch *zerfällen* werden.

the fact that it's impossible to really like someone who puts his feelings on show. They then become too corporeal and are too likely to feign selflessness.

But if we consider the emotional impact Rousseau has had on others, he appears immeasurably great, and it is of almost no consequence what effect his feelings had on himself.

There are certain *simple* qualities inherent in human beings for which one could sell one's soul.

How handsome he becomes in remorse! But for whose benefit? Only the observer's.

He feels like a thief of the world. Soon there will be nothing left for him to marvel at.

Depreciation through repetition. Excitement through repetition?

My greatest experience after Büchner was William Blake, in England.
My earliest childhood experience was Swift, in that same country.
England, for me, lies between Swift and Blake.

From here on, you will be given no new places. But how the old ones *gain in strength!* They virtually bury themselves in the ground, they send for you, they draw you to them, they call out, they scream, and it is very likely that they will, belatedly, *split you apart.*

Jules Renard, in seinem ›Journal‹, hat mir etwas wiedergegeben, was ich lange verloren hatte: die Unschuld der Franzosen.

Etwas an den Juden bleibt staunenswert: ihre vernichtende Beschimpfung durch die Propheten.
Ein Volk, das solche Beschimpfungen in seinen Glaubenskanon aufnimmt!

Aber ich habe nichts satt.
Ich bin immer noch im Leben enthalten. Ich sage nicht: endlich. Ich kapituliere nicht. Es ist erniedrigend zu sterben und nicht zu wissen, ob in hundert Jahren noch ein Mensch da ist.
Es war leichter damals, mit der sicheren Aussicht auf die Hölle zu sterben. *Diese* Aussicht auf keinen Menschen in faßbarer Zeit ist das Furchtbarste, was es je gegeben hat.

Nichts, nichts, nichts, und um alles tut's mir noch leid, am meisten um die herrlichen Mythen und Geschichten. Daß sie, das Beste an uns, wegen uns verschwinden sollen, reizt mich bis zur Tollwut.
Wem kann man sie anvertrauen? Wer hebt sie zum Überwintern auf? Wer wiederholt sie von Zeit zu Zeit, daß sie durch Vergessensein nicht in Auflösung geraten?

Laß dir den *Ton* der Hoffnung von niemand vorschreiben.

»– ... denn ich bin der Reden so voll, daß mich der Odem in meinem Inneren ängstet.«

Hiob, 32, 18

With his *Journal* Jules Renard returned to me something I had lost a long time ago: the innocence of the French.

There is something about the Jews that continues to be amazing: their prophets' scathing castigation of them. What a people—to include such reviling of themselves in their articles of faith!

No, I can't get enough of anything!
I am still contained within life. I do not say: at last. I do not capitulate. It is humiliating to die without knowing whether a single human being will still be around in a hundred years. Dying used to be easier with the certain prospect of hell. But *this* prospect of no people left within the foreseeable future is the most horrible notion that ever was.

Nothing, nothing, nothing, and yet I still painfully miss everything, most of all the marvelous myths and tales. That these, the best in us, are doomed to vanish—because of us —that enrages me to the point of madness.
To whom could they be entrusted? Who will keep them safe through the winter? Who will repeat them from time to time, so that they may not disintegrate through being forgotten?

Do not let anyone dictate to you the *tonality* of hope.

" . . . for I am so full of the spoken word that I am fearful of the spirit's breath within me."

Job 32:18

Jeremias, der die Kinderspuren sah, sich auf den Boden warf und sie küßte.

Heute?

Der hartnäckige Widerstand gegen die Bibel, der mich Jahrzehnte von ihr ferngehalten hat, hängt damit zusammen, daß ich meiner Herkunft nie nachgeben wollte. Wo immer ich die Bibel aufschlug, schien sie mir vertraut. Sie war es besonders dann, wenn ich auf eine Stelle stieß, die ich nicht kannte. Diese *innere* Vertrautheit erfüllte mich mit Mißtrauen. Ich wollte nicht ein geistiges Leben führen, das von vornherein festgesetzt war, ich wollte kein *vorgegebenes* geistiges Leben. Ich wollte mich immer wieder überraschen und überwältigen lassen und dadurch allmählich zum Freund und Kenner alles Menschlichen werden. Das Übergewicht des Biblischen, das die Welt solange geprägt hat, durfte ich nicht einfach hinnehmen. Ich mußte mir genug Gegengewichte verschaffen, bevor ich mich der Bibel auslieferte.

Ich glaube, daß es jetzt so weit ist, und daß ich ohne Scham und ohne Eitelkeit der Bibel nachgeben kann. Ich will sie jetzt in jeder Verborgenheit kennenlernen und mir nichts von ihr entgehen lassen. Ich will sie fassen und gegen die Mythen aller Völker halten, von denen ich erfüllt bin. Ich will ihre Weisheit so auf mich wirken lassen, als sei sie nicht ohnehin schon verborgen in mir da. Ich will die Bibel *ausliefern* und dadurch erfahren.

Sein Gedächtnis ließ nach und er wurde zum Dichter. Seit er nach seinen Eindrücken und Erinnerungen suchen mußte, wurden sie unerwartet und fremd. Im Dunkel gewannen sie Farbe. Er mußte weit langen, um sie zu erreichen. Sie waren nicht gleich da. Sie wurden dringlicher, indem sie sich versagten, lockerer, indem sie in Schlaf versanken. Wenn sie erwachten, waren sie in ein gefährliches Licht getaucht, das er nie er-

Jeremiah, seeing that children had walked on the ground, threw himself down to kiss their tracks.
Today?

My stubborn resistance to the Bible, which kept me away from it for decades, has to do with the fact that I never wanted to submit to my origin. Wherever I opened the Bible, it seemed familiar to me, particularly when I happened on a passage I had not known. This *innate* intimacy filled me with distrust. I did not wish to lead a spiritual life which had been previously determined. I did not want a *preordained* spiritual life. I wanted to let myself be surprised and overwhelmed time and time again and thereby gradually become a friend of and an expert on everything human. I simply could not accept the great weight of the biblical tradition which has left its imprint on the world for so long, I had to secure a sufficiently heavy counterweight before surrendering to the Bible.
I think I have reached now a point where I may yield to the Bible without shame or vanity. I now wish to discover it, in all its concealments, without missing a thing. I wish to grasp it and hold it up against the myths of all the nations, the myths that have kept me sated. I wish to experience the effect of its wisdom, as if it were not already concealed within me. I wish to *forsake* the Bible, so as to experience it fully.

His memory diminished and he became a poet. Ever since he had to struggle to find his impressions and memories, these became unexpected and strange. In darkness they gained color. He had to stretch far to reach them. They did not appear right away. They became more urgent as they kept their distance, and they loosened up only as they sank into sleep. When they awoke, they were bathed in a dan-

kannte. Er mußte sich sagen, daß er sich bis ins hohe Alter nicht gekannt hatte und gewann – sehr spät – den *Durst des Staunens*. Denn was war das früher für ein Staunen gewesen, das einen anheimelte! Zu einem Trunkenbold des Schreckens wurde er jetzt und prüfte sich endlich, daß die Funken stoben.

Es wird ihm unbehaglich zumute, wenn seine Gedanken *wörtlich* genommen werden.

Auseinanderhalten, die Sätze auseinanderhalten, sonst werden sie zu Farbe.

Seine Wahrhaftigkeit liegt in der Übertreibung. Er lügt, wenn er nicht übertreibt.

Demut, eine späte Nachgeburt.

Der Tod der Aphorismen ist ihre Gleichartigkeit, die verwechselbare Gestalt. Verwelkt, bevor sie einen Atemzug getan haben. Gegensatz: das Aushauchen Jouberts.

Am wenigsten bist du der, den du rühmst. Darum rühmst du ihn doch, weil du gern wie er *wärest*.

Zweierlei Selbstdarstellung: durch Erinnerung oder durch Einfälle. Beide sind legitim. Aber handeln sie vom selben Menschen?

gerous light, which he was never able to recognize. He had to admit that he had not known himself until very old age and only very late did he gain the *thirst* for wonder. For what kind of wonder had that been that made him feel at home? Now, however, he was bold with intoxication, eager for every terrifying amazement, and in the end he put himself to such tests as to make the sparks fly!

He feels uncomfortable if his thoughts are taken *literally*.

Keep things apart, keep sentences separate, or else they turn into colors.

His truthfulness lies in his exaggeration. Whenever he does not exaggerate, he lies.

Humbleness: a late afterbirth.

The death of aphorisms lies in their similarity, their all too confusable form. Wilted even before having taken their first breath. In opposition: Joubert breathing his last.

You are least of all like the one you praise. Yet you praise him nevertheless, because you wish you *were* like him.

Two kinds of self-description: one through memory, one through inspiration. Both are legitimate. But do they apply to the same person?

Dauerläufer: erträgt keinen Schatten auf seinem Schatten.

Ein Leben aus *einem einzigen* Briefe.

Kannst du dem seine Einsamkeit zugute halten, der um ihret-
willen die Welt zerstört?

Heimlich wärmt das Vergessene.

»Die ihr eigenes Naturell bewahrt haben, sind immer über das
anderer entzückt, auch wenn es im Gegensatz zu dem ihren
steht.« *Joubert*

Der hat zwei Sprachen: in einer sehr hochgebauschten preist
er einige rare Preiswürdige, plündert sie, schmeichelt ihnen,
immer auf erhabenster Ebene, und es ist, als käme seine Sprache stracks aus einem Überhimmel und besäße keine irdi-
schen Worte. In der anderen spricht er von denselben, aber so,
als wären sie niedrig wie er und hätten nur Niederträchtiges
von sich gegeben. Er ergötzt sich an der Weise, wie das Leben
ihnen mitgespielt hat, er taucht und badet sie in Neid und
Ekel. Das aber schreibt er nie auf, er schreibt nur in der anderen, der Preis-Sprache.

Was ist Erinnerung?
Man macht, was man war.
Das klingt so, als wäre man frei, es zu machen. Das ist man
aber gar nicht, denn man erfindet nichts. Man macht Schritte
und glaubt sie frei zu bestimmen, aber sobald sie gemacht
sind, spürt man, daß sie vorgezeichnet waren.

Long-distance runner: he cannot bear a shadow on his shadow.

A life from *one single* letter.

Can you make allowances for someone who, for the sake of solitude, is willing to destroy the world?

All that we have forgotten secretly keeps us warm.

"Those who have kept their own personality are always enchanted by that of others, even if it is in opposition to their own."   *Joubert*

This man has two languages: a high-flown, fanciful one with which he praises, plunders, and flatters a very few praise-worthy people, always on the most refined level and as if his language emanated directly from some kind of super-heaven and was devoid of all secular words. In his second language he describes the very same persons, but as if they were as low as he himself and as if all they had produced were utterly base. He delights in their misfortunes, he drenches and bathes them in envy and contempt. But this he never records, for he only writes in the other language, the one reserved for laudation.

What is memory?
One does what one was.
This sounds as if we were free to do so. But this is not the case at all, for we do not invent anything. We take a few steps and believe that we have determined them freely, but as soon as we have taken them we realize that they were really predetermined.

Erst was durch Erinnerung gegangen ist, läßt sich wiedererkennen.

Das Traurige der Erinnerung: was sie verbraucht hat.

Das Heitere der Erinnerung: der Überschuß.

In der *Steuerung* besteht die Kunst der Erinnerung.

Was man beiseite liegen läßt, was man umgeht.

Das Rare und das Gehäufte.

Was sich vordrängt: entstellte Figuren, die sich berichtigen müssen. Wie kommt es, daß man manches am Leben halten will und anderes gar nicht?

Das Verdünnte will sich runden, durch Sprechen. Aus einem einzigen Wort sollen wieder alle Sätze werden. Zusammenhänge, die man zum erstenmal begreift. Die Unwürdigkeit amorpher Aneinanderreihung. Was man anderen getan hat, holt sie zum Leben herauf. Man ist ein Schuldner wie aus vielen Existenzen, obwohl man nur diese eine gelebt hat.

Jeder Mensch weiß mehr, als sich in einem neuen langen Leben erzählen ließe.

Wovon ist die Auswahl bestimmt? Von einer einzigen Farbe des Gefühls: von Dankbarkeit oder Bitterkeit, Sehnsucht oder Haß.

In einer anderen Sprache würde man sich anders erinnern. Das wäre genauer zu untersuchen, und bist du nicht eben der Richtige, es zu tun?

Lob des Alters

Ein Alter zu erreichen, das man sich wünscht, nicht weil es ein ideales Alter gibt, sondern weil man die Vorstellung loswerden soll, daß es ein Alter gibt, das für alle zu bevorzugen wäre.

Diese Vorstellung habe ich nie gehabt. Erfahrung wollte ich, die Kenntnis nämlich vieler Menschen, Zeit zu dieser Kenntnis, sodaß man sie immer wieder bedenken kann, nach langen Pausen, in denen sie vielleicht für einen verschwunden waren.

Es ist eine wunderbare Vorstellung, ein- und denselben Menschen zehn- oder zwölfmal zu kennen, ihm so oft zu begeg-

Only that which once has passed through memory can be recognized again.

The sadness of memory: what it has used up.

The joy of memory: its surplus.

The art of memory consists in its *control.*

What one leaves aside and what one circumvents.

The rare and the piled-up.

What pushes to the fore: distorted figures who need to rectify themselves. Why is it that we wish to keep some things alive and others not at all?

The diluted seeks to round itself out by means of speech. All sentences are to emerge once more from a single word. Connections understood for the first time. The unworthiness of amorphous agglomerations. What we have done to others calls them back to life. We are all in debt as if from several existences, even though we have lived only this particular life.

Each person knows more than could be told in the course of a long new life.

What determines the selection? A single emotional color: gratefulness or bitterness, longing or hatred. In a different language we would remember in a different way. This should be investigated more thoroughly, and aren't you just the right one to undertake this?

In praise of old age
To reach the age we desire, not because there is such a thing as an ideal age, but because we should get rid of the notion that there is one age which is ideal for everyone. I have never adhered to that notion. I myself wanted experience—that is, the acquaintance of many people, the time to acquire that acquaintance, the time to ponder it over and over, following long intervals during which the people themselves may have vanished from my life. What a wonderful idea to get to know one person ten or twelve times, to meet him each

nen, als habe man ihn nie gekannt, aber ohne die Erinnerung
an ihn verloren zu haben, ihn *mit sich*, nicht nur mit anderen
zu vergleichen. Die Tradition, die ein Mensch in einem ge-
winnt, durch die Jahre, in denen man von ihm gewußt hat, genügt nämlich nicht. Sie setzt Rost an, und dazu sollte einem
jeder Mensch zu gut sein. Wohl aber gibt es die Möglichkeit,
daß der Einzelne sich für einen zu dem Vielfachen bündelt,
das er ja auf alle Fälle ist, und dazu braucht man neue Begegnungen mit ihm, nach langen Pausen. In anderen Worten
würde das bedeuten, daß man sich nie an einen Menschen gewöhnt. Daß man über ihn staunt, als hätte er sich einem noch
nie dargestellt, einem nichts angetan, einen nicht beglückt.
Die Erwartung, die man jedem neuen Menschen entgegen-
bringt, hätte man dann auch für solche, die man schon vor
Jahrzehnten gekannt hat.
Für diesen Prozeß einer Vervielfachung der einzelnen Menschen braucht man ein langes Leben. Es mag viele Nachteile
haben, alt zu sein. Es hat unvergleichlich größere Vorteile.
Da ist zum Beispiel das Wagnis der Erinnerung. Man darf sich
ihr hingeben, ohne Götzenkult mit sich zu betreiben. Es ist
ein unendlicher Reichtum an Dingen da, die alle zu erforschen
wären. Unerschöpflich die Welt, die der Mensch aufgenommen hat, phantastisch die Formen, die Dinge in ihm angenommen haben. Selbst die Entstellungen haben ihre Wahrheit,
wenn sie nur klar genug gefaßt werden.
Ein anderer Nutzen, für den ich dieses kalte Wort nicht
scheue, wäre die Prüfung der Moralgesetze, die einem früh
eingesagt wurden, nach denen man im großen und ganzen gelebt hat. Stimmen sie? Oder sind sie nicht fein genug? Bedür-
fen sie einer Korrektur? Wie soll man das wissen, ohne ihre
Erfahrung über lange Strecken der Zeit und ohne Einsicht in
diese Erfahrung?
Selbst der furchtbarste Nachteil eines langen Lebens, das was
daran so entsetzlich erscheint, daß man sich manchmal versucht fühlen könnte, es darum allein zu beenden – die Tatsache, daß man so viele überlebt hat, ist nicht ganz so hoff-

time as if it were the first, yet without having lost the remembrance of him, to compare him not merely with others
but *with himself.* The fact that over the years each person
becomes a tradition is not enough. For this tradition begins
to rust, and no one should be left to such a fate. In fact, it
is possible that this individual might, in our perception,
multiply into the manifold being which he actually is, but
this requires new encounters separated by long intervals of
time. In other words, this would mean that we never fully
get used to someone. We would continue to be astounded
by him as if he had never made our acquaintance, as if he
had never done us any harm or made us happy. The expectations reserved for any new acquaintance then also
would be directed toward those whom we have known for
decades.

But this "multiplication" of individuals requires a long life.
There may be many disadvantages to being old, but there
are incomparably greater benefits.

There is, for instance, the daring adventure of remembering:
we may indulge in it without running the risk of idolizing
ourselves. The wealth of things to be explored is infinite.
Inexhaustible the world to be absorbed by an individual,
fantastic the forms that things have assumed in his mind.
Even the distortions contain their own truth, provided they
are grasped with sufficient stringency.

Another benefit (and I do not hesitate to use this cold term)
consists in a critical examination of the moral codes which
were imprinted on us at an early age and which, by and
large, have guided our lives. Are these precepts true? Or are
they not fine-tuned enough? Do they need to be amended?
How would it be possible to answer these questions without
a sizable body of experience and the insights gained from
that experience?

Even the worst drawback of a long life, that one has outlived
so many others—a fact so horrifying we are drawn toward
suicide—is not quite as hopeless as we might think at first.

nungslos, wie man denkt. Man kann nämlich die, die vor einem gestorben sind, zu ihrem Leben zurückholen, indem man sie darstellt. Das allerdings ist nicht eine Sache der freien Wahl, das zu tun ist eine oberste Schuldigkeit, und nur wer die Toten so darstellt, wie sie wirklich waren, ohne Abstrich und ohne Verklärung, der ist vor dem Schicksal derer geschützt, die sich an denen, die sie überlebt haben, *mästen*.

Das Alter ist eine Reduktion nur für den, der es nicht verdient. Man verdient es, indem man sich nicht zurückzieht, oder nur als Wechsel zu einer strengeren und anspruchsvolleren Form von Leistung. Sie setzt ein Leben für alle voraus, die gescheitert sind, aber auch für alle, von denen man spürt, daß sie vielleicht nicht scheitern werden. Ich möchte das das doppelte, das Janus-Gesicht des Alters nennen: das eine ist den Geschlagenen zugewandt, das andere denen, die noch nicht, ja vielleicht nie zu schlagen waren.

Nochmals: Zum Alter

Die Gelegenheit wird einem gegeben, manches wiedergutzumachen. Die immer gefährlichere Verfassung, in der die Welt sich findet, wie wirkt sie auf das Alter ein?

Alles Vergebliche. Vorsicht und Nachsicht.

Wie wirkt sich das Alter auf die Worte aus?

Sie werden einem sonderbar, als hätten sie ein Bewußtsein davon, daß sie nicht mehr ungezählte Male ausgesprochen werden.

Das Überwältigende neuer Freundschaften: der Aufwand, den sie machen, die Kraft, die sie aufbringen müssen, um sich gegen alte zu halten.

Es ist alles kostbarer, vielleicht weil es gezählt ist. Wunderbare Vergeblichkeit des Lernens zu keinem Zweck mehr, es ist nur Lernen an sich. Was man erlernt, dient nicht mehr der Expansion. An Sprachen macht man sich bloß heran, weil man sie nicht mehr sprechen wird, bestimmte Gedanken hat man, bloß weil es unwahrscheinlich geworden ist, daß sie sich wiederholen.

For it is possible to fetch those others back to life by depicting them. But this is not a matter of free choice. To do so is our highest moral obligation and only those who depict the dead as they truly were—without shortchanging but also without glorifying them—will be spared the fate of those who *gorge themselves* on the people they survived.

Old age is a reduction only for those who do not deserve it. Old age is deserved by anyone who refuses to abdicate, who compels himself to follow a more severe and exacting standard for his actions. It presupposes a life dedicated to all those who have foundered, but also to all those whom we expect not to fail. I would call that the twin face, the Janus face of old age: one side is turned toward the defeated, while the other side is turned toward those who have not yet been defeated and perhaps never could be.

And once more: On old age
We are granted the opportunity to make amends for a great many things. The ever more dangerous state of our world, how does it affect old age?

All is futile. Prudence and forbearance.

How does old age affect words?

They begin to sound strange to us, as if they themselves had some premonition that they will no longer be uttered in infinite iteration.

What is overwhelming in new friendships: the expansiveness of their efforts, the strength they need to muster, so as to maintain themselves against older established friendships.

Everything becomes more valuable, maybe because it is numbered. The wondrous futility of learning devoid of purpose: it is learning for its own sake. What we master no longer serves any expansion. We study new languages only because we will no longer have an opportunity to speak them; we have certain thoughts merely because we will probably never repeat them.

Das Nutzbare verliert an Bedeutung. Die Dinge bedeuten nur noch sie selbst.

Zwei Tendenzen, die sich nur scheinbar widersprechen, kennzeichnen die Zeit: die Anbetung der Jugend und das *Absterben* der Erfahrung.

Es gibt auch welche, die mit der Nichtigkeit des Lebens auftrumpfen und daraus eine unersättliche Anmaßung beziehen. Die den anderen nur als Gegenstand der Beschimpfung kennen, während sie jeden Abschaum ihres eigenen Rechts mit Zähnen und Klauen verteidigen. Man frägt sich, was aus solchen im Alter werden könnte: vielleicht Friedhofbesitzer.

Gegen die Anbetung der Jugend wäre nichts einzuwenden, solange es nicht die Jugend selber ist, die sich anbetet.

Die Darstellung des Absterbens, mehr als einem gelungen, scheint mir erschöpft. Es bleibt nun nur noch *ein* origineller Vorwurf: die Darstellung ihrer Verhinderung, ihrer bewußten Umwendung ins Gegenteil.

Für das Alter ließe sich sagen, daß es die Kostbarkeit des Lebens steigert.

Wer in einer Krankheit darum gekämpft hat, sich Schritt um Schritt und Qual um Qual das Leben zurückgeholt hat, der erst weiß ganz, was es wert ist. Mein höchster Respekt gilt denen, die sich ihr Leben wieder erworben haben.

Man sollte es wünschen, und es stünde besser um die Welt, wenn jedem diese Chance sozusagen offiziell einmal gegeben wäre. Statt dessen gibt es die läppischen, ewig fortgesetzten, tausendmal wiederholten Gesundheitsübungen der ohnehin Gesunden.

Der Hauptnachteil des Alters, und ein so großer, daß er beinahe alle Vorteile aufwiegt, ist, daß man kaum mehr an die anderen denkt.

Dagegen ist ein Kraut gewachsen: es heißt Unentbehrlichkeit. Was man weiß, das niemand weiß, was man sagt, das niemand sagen kann. Es soll so viel davon da sein, daß die anderen es spüren, es haben wollen und einen nicht in Ruhe lassen. Ihr

What is useful loses in importance. Things only mean what they are in themselves.

Two trends, which only apparently contradict each other, epitomize this era: the worship of youth and the *extinction* of experience.

There are also those who boast about the futility of life and draw from it an insatiable presumption. They recognize all others merely as objects of vilification, while they defend their own scummy rights with fangs and claws. One wonders what really does happen to such individuals in old age: perhaps they become graveyard owners.

There is no objection to the worship of youth—as long as it is not youth which is worshipping itself.

The portrayal of extinction—in which many have been successful—has been exhausted by now, at least to my mind. There is only *one* truly original theme left: how to thwart this extinction and how to turn it into its opposite.

In favor of old age we may assert that it heightens the value of life.

Only he who has struggled in sickness to recapture life, step by step and in pain and suffering, truly knows its worth. My highest respect is reserved for those who thus have regained their life.

Everyone should be granted—so to speak, by official decree —at least one opportunity to do so, for then the world would be in better shape. But instead we are confronted with the foolish, incessant, and infinitely repeated fitness exercises of those who are already fit and hale.

The main drawback of old age, one which practically outweighs all its advantages, is the fact that we hardly think of others at all.

However, there exists a remedy for this: indispensability. To know what no one else knows, to be able to say what no one else can say. There must be enough of this so that it is felt by the others, so that they clamor for it and refuse to leave us in peace. Their demands serve as a challenge,

Verlangen dient als Herausforderung, es zwingt einen zu reagieren, und indem man es hergibt, bezieht man sich doch auf die anderen.

Es ist also zu empfehlen, Alte nicht in Ruhe zu lassen, auf kluge Weise, die zu Ergebnissen führt, aber unablässig.

Mit der Rechthaberei ist es schwierig: am besten ist es, sie zu umgehen. Eine frontale Herausforderung ist hier nutzlos, eine sterilere Form des Kampfes ist fast nicht auszudenken.

Es mag lächerlich klingen, daß ein Alter davon spricht, wozu Alte noch nütz sind und wozu ganz unnütz, aber was ich sage, stammt nicht von heute, ich spreche aus sehr langer Erfahrung: Alte haben mich immer, schon in frühester Jugend, fasziniert; als Kind bin ich ihnen nachgerannt und habe über sie gestaunt und die, die viel zu erzählen hatten, hätte ich am liebsten am Rocksaum für immer festgehalten. Fassungslos war ich über die, die zu faul waren, etwas zu erzählen, das waren dann die falschen Alten, die, die sich bloß so ausstaffiert hatten, als ob sie's wären.

Nichts wäre ich lieber gewesen als ein richtiger Alter, und so wie manche sich wünschen reich zu werden und an nichts anderes denken, bis es ihnen gelingt, so war mein heftigster Wunsch der, alt zu werden.

»... et je ne puis approuver que ceux qui cherchent en gémissant.«   *Pascal*

»Tout ce qui est incompréhensible ne laisse pas d'être.«   *Pascal*

Was wäre Isaak Babel später geworden? Nach aller Angst, nach der Geschicklichkeit des Entkommens?
Über geduckte Menschen hat man kein Urteil.

they force us to react, and by acceding to them, we, the older, end up relating to the younger.

Consequently, it is advisable to pursue old people, intelligently, in a way that leads to results, but doggedly.

Admittedly, the fact that old people claim to know everything better poses a problem: the best solution is to circumvent it. A frontal challenge is senseless, a more sterile form of confrontation is hard to imagine.

It may seem somewhat ludicrous that an old man should take it upon himself to suggest how the old may still be useful and how not, but what I am saying here did not just pop into my head this morning; it is based on very long experience. Old people have always fascinated me, even in my earliest childhood; in those days I used to run after them and was full of wonder at their very existence; and the ones who had much to tell, I would have liked to grab by their coattails and hold on to forever. The ones who were too lazy to spin tales left me perplexed; those were false old people, who had merely bedizened themselves to seem old. I wanted nothing more than to be a genuine old man myself, and as some wish to become rich and think of nothing else until they have achieved their goal, so my own intense desire was to grow old.

" . . . et je ne puis approuver que ceux qui cherchent en gémissant."   *Pascal*

"Tout ce qui est incompréhensible ne laisse pas d'être."
                                                                                                           Pascal

What would Isaac Babel have turned out to be later on? After all the fear and the cleverness shown in his escape? One does not judge men bowed by fate.

Im Grunde besteht seine Freiheit nur darin, daß er keine Befehle entgegennimmt und sich niemandem unterordnet.
Ist das aber nicht eben die Freiheit der Machthaber? Nein, diese erteilen selbst Befehle und betrachten alle anderen als untergeordnet.

Er atmet zu lang, um einen Hauch zu lang, und diesen Hauch empfindet er als seine Seele.

Er spuckt jeden an. Auch sich. Das nennt er seine Wahrheit.

Ohne geliehene Leben hält niemand es aus, das eigene genügt nicht.

Was einer von *sich* sagt, im Tagebuch, ist schon darum wahrer als alles Geschwätz der anderen, weil er es für eine lange Verborgenheit sagt, in der es wahr *wird*.
Die anderen werfen ihr Gerede hin, und es ist auf der Stelle unwahr.

Es wird ihm schwerfallen, sich von Goethe zu trennen. Er hat sich so viel von ihm aufgespart. Er verteilt ihn an immer spätere Jahre.

»C'est un grand signe de médiocrité de louer toujours modérément.«

Vauvenargues

Alles, was er angekündigt hat, bringt ihn zum Schweigen.

Basically, his freedom consists only in his refusal to accept all orders and to subordinate himself to anyone.
But is this not the freedom of the powerful? No, because they issue orders and they treat everyone else as their subordinates.

His breathing is too long, too long by a single breath, and it is this breath which he perceives as being his soul.

He spits on everyone, including himself. This he calls truth.

Everybody needs to borrow a few lives; one life just isn't enough.

What somebody says about *himself* in his journal is bound to be truer than all the babbling of others, if for no other reason than because he intends it for a long period of concealment, during which it *will become* true.
The others throw their twaddle about, and it turns untrue on the spot.

It will be difficult for him to part from Goethe. He has saved up so much of him, and keeps allocating his savings for increasingly advanced years.

"C'est un grand signe de médiocrité de louer toujours modérément."

Vauvenargues

All that he has predicted makes him fall silent.

Was du gegen den Tod zu sagen hast, ist nicht weniger unwirklich als die Seelen-Unsterblichkeit der Religionen. Es ist sogar noch unwirklicher, denn es will *alles* bewahren, nicht nur eine Seele.

Eine Unersättlichkeit, die beinahe nicht zu begreifen ist.

Your tirade against death is no less unreal than the immortality of souls proclaimed by various religions. In fact, it is even less real, for it seeks to preserve *everything*—not just a single soul.

This insatiability almost surpasses all understanding.

VIII

Mühsal des Cervantes im ehrzerfressenen Spanien. Spätes Werk, nach fünfzig, und viel spätere höchste Ehren. Soldat und Sklave jung, während fünf Jahren das Niederste und darin sich bewährend, mit vierzig Steuereintreiber und darin scheiternd, von einer Familie geplagt wie von Läusen, ihr – dank Schreiben – nicht erliegend, auch im Schreiben nicht zu begrenzen, an Erlebtem so reich, daß sein Geschriebenes nie erstickt.

Zum ›Größten‹ gehört insbesondere alles Unrecht, das er getan hat, wenn er es *weiß*.

Einen Menschen stundenlang anhören, in der festen Absicht, ihn nicht zu erhören, ihn um sein Leben reden hören (selber in Sicherheit, Ruhe und Glanz) – gibt es etwas Niederträchtigeres?

Mit Philosophen, die in sich selbst verwirkt sind, kann er nichts anfangen. Er braucht Philosophen, die Lebenspunkte in ihm oder anderen schmerzlich berühren.

Abneigung gegen die Abstammungslehre. Wo immer ich auf sie stoße, fühle ich eine Art von Lähmung. Sie erscheint mir so unglaubwürdig wie die Lehre von einer Schöpfung, und jedenfalls farbloser.
Es wird alles der breitesten Zeit zugeschrieben, in Abständen, die wir nie empfinden können. Als Sprungfeder für die Bewährung neuer Formen wird das Überleben eingesetzt, so

VIII

The hardships of Cervantes in honor-corroded Spain. A late oeuvre, when he was past fifty, and much later, the highest honors. A soldier and slave in his youth, for five years on the lowest social rung and nevertheless proving his worth there, a failed tax collector at forty, tormented by his family as by lice, yet not succumbing to it thanks to his writing, irrepressible in his writing as well, his experience so rich that his writing never chokes.

The "greatest" man must also be measured by all the wrong he has done, provided he is *conscious* of it.

Can there be anything more despicable than to listen for hours to a man with the firm intention of not giving in to his pleadings, to listen to him begging for his life—all the while enjoying safety, comfort, and splendor?

He has no use for philosophers who are involved with themselves exclusively. He needs philosophers who painfully touch his own vital points or those of others.

Aversion to the theory of origin of the species. Wherever I encounter it, I feel a kind of paralysis. It appears to me just as implausible as the story of the Creation and, in any case, much less colorful.
Everything is being attributed to the broadest spans of time, in intervals so large as to be beyond our grasp. The acid test for the qualifying of new forms is their survival per se, so

wird der Massentod zu etwas Nützlichem. Damit etwas Neues entsteht, muß unendlich viel Leben zugrundegehen, eine monströse Vorstellung, die im Grunde dem Bereiche der Macht entspringt.

Daß man sich Leute viel älter, als sie geworden sind, nicht vorstellen kann.
So wie es Jugendbilder, echte, gibt, müßten sich fiktive Altersbilder finden.

Die Tatsachen-Historiker, die an der Geschichte eben das verloren geben, was interessant ist: ihre Erfindung.

Lob belebt den Geist, der sich's nachträglich verdienen möchte.

Die beiden Zeitgenossen Cervantes und Shakespeare: vom einen weiß man so viel und vom anderen nichts. Was wären sie, wenn sich Wissen und Unwissen von ihnen vertauschen ließen?

»Ein junger Salvadorianer zum Beispiel marschierte Bahnschienen entlang von El Salvador bis in die USA, weil zu Hause seine Eltern und drei Schwestern mitten auf dem Dorfplatz erschossen worden waren.«

Darf man einen einzelnen Menschen so ernst nehmen, daß er für alle anderen steht?
Darf man ihn mit so viel Liebe und so viel Unschuld beladen?

that mass death becomes something useful. In order for anything new to emerge, a great deal of life must first perish—this is a monstrous concept which essentially originates in the realm of power.

That it should be impossible to imagine people much older than they actually have become.
Just as there are pictures of people in their youth, genuine ones, there should also exist fictive pictures of people in their old age.

The historians of facts who omit the most interesting thing about history—namely, its invention.

Praise first animates the spirit, which then desires to deserve it.

Two contemporaries, Cervantes and Shakespeare: we know so much about one and nothing at all about the other. Who would they be if we could interchange that knowledge and that ignorance?

"A young Salvadoran, for example, walked up the railway tracks all the way from El Salvador to the United States because at home his parents and three of his sisters had been shot in the middle of the village square."

May a single individual be taken so seriously as to stand for all others?
May he be burdened with so much love and so much innocence?

Die Laute der Wale: Im Grunde empfinde ich Scham, diese friedlichen Laute von Geschöpfen zu hören, die sich gegen uns nicht zur Wehr setzen können. Wir haben uns nicht nur wie von allen ihren Leib, wir haben uns auch ihre Regungen füreinander zugeeignet, doch dürfen wir sie zur Strafe nicht verstehen. Ich *verzichte* darauf, weiter in sie einzudringen. Ich lasse ab von ihnen. Mein Mitgefühl für sie ist vergiftet. Sie *bleiben* Beute.

Finde die Schmerzen, die du *bereitet* hast, die erlittenen bewahren sich, ohne daß du dich einmischst.

Es beruhigt ihn, daß er die Namen der Tiere nennt. Er ist stolz auf ihre Namen. »Den gibt es. Den haben wir doch nicht ausgerottet.«

Er wendet sich allem zu, das nie mehr sein wird. Er findet eine unauslöschliche Gegenwart. Er legt den Finger an sie, sie lacht auf und zerstiebt.

Klagen? Warten. Warten. Zu Ende gewartet.
Das geduldige Geschöpf, der Mensch. Das rasende Geschöpf, der Mensch. Das verzehrende, das verzehrte Geschöpf, der Mensch.

Die Weisheit des Erwachens. Nach dem Schlaf, unmittelbar danach, denkt es sich anders. Schwebend, weniger gewichtig, durchsichtig, selbstlos, leise.

The sounds of whales: Basically I feel ashamed at eavesdropping on those peaceable sounds of creatures who are defenseless against us. Not only did we appropriate their bodies—as we did with all the rest—we also took the emotions they display toward each other—though we are being punished for it by being unable to understand them. I myself *renounce* all further investigation of them. I will let them be. My compassion for them has been poisoned. They *remain* prey.

Find the pains you have *inflicted*. Those you have suffered will keep well enough without any effort on your part.

It soothes him to utter the names of the animals. He is proud of their names. "This one is still around. We haven't exterminated it yet."

He turns his attention toward everything that will never again exist. He finds an inextinguishable presence. He puts his finger to it and it bursts into laughter and scatters in all directions.

To mourn? To wait. To wait. To have waited till the end. Man, the patient creature. Man, the raging creature. The creature devouring, the creature devoured: Man.

The wisdom of awakening. After sleep, immediately thereafter, one's thinking is different. Floating, less weighty, transparent, selfless, quiet.

Carlyle über seine Träume.

»Träume! Meine Träume sind immer unangenehm – nichts als Konfusion – Verlieren der Kleider und Ähnliches, nichts Schönes. Dieselben Träume Nacht für Nacht wieder, über eine lange Zeit. Ich bin ein *schlechterer* Mann in meinen Träumen als wach – begehe feige Handlungen, träume davon, daß ich für ein Verbrechen belangt werde. Ich bin lang schon zum Schluß gekommen, daß Träume für mich von keinerlei Bedeutung sind.«

William Allingham, A Diary

Zu voll, drei Bände Lebensgeschichte haben ihn nicht entlastet, seither ist mehr Vergangenheit in ihm da als zuvor. In alle Richtungen wächst die Vergangenheit, durch ihre Darstellung. Müßte dasselbe nicht für Geschichte gelten? Oder ist die Geschichtsschreibung reduktiv, im Gegensatz zur gestalteten Erinnerung?

»Der Mensch muß wieder ruiniert werden«, ein Satz Goethes, der des Härtesten, der Prädestination des Augustin würdig wäre. Wie leicht bildet sich dieser Satz im Geiste eines Menschen, wenn er Napoleon und Mozart im selben Atemzug nennt!

Wohl gibt es Tiere, die Menschen durch ihren Stumpfsinn ähneln. Aber nie wird man das Gefühl los, daß der Stumpfsinn von Tieren es nicht wirklich ist und jedenfalls unschuldiger ist als der unsere.

Das Zaumzeug der Worte. Es soll sie leicht schmerzen, aber so, daß sie dafür noch dankbar sind.

Carlyle about his dreams:

"Dreams! My dreams are always unpleasant—nothing but confusion—loss of clothes and similar things, nothing beautiful. The same dreams night after night, over a long span of time. I am a *worse* man in my dreams than when awake —I commit cowardly deeds. I dream that I am being prosecuted for some crime. Long ago I have come to the conclusion that dreams have no significance for me."

William Allingham, A Diary

He is too full: even three volumes of his life story have failed to relieve him; there is more past inside him now than ever before. The past grows in all directions through its depiction. Wouldn't the same hold true for history? Or is historiography reductive, in contrast to memory accumulated and shaped?

"Mankind need be destroyed once more." A sentence by Goethe, every bit as tough as Augustine's predestination. How readily this thought forms in the mind of anyone who mentions Napoleon and Mozart in the same breath!

It is true that there are animals that resemble Man in their stupidity. Yet one cannot help feeling that this stupidity of animals is not real and that, in any case, it is more innocent than ours.

Putting a bridle on words: It should cause them some slight pain, but in a way that would still make them grateful for it.

Wie man zu etwas wird, indem man es immerzu nennt. Karl Kraus sagt so lange, Jahre und Jahre, zu sich Swift, bis er es schließlich in den ›Letzten Tagen der Menschheit‹ wird.

Vorurteile soll man nicht einfach los werden. Nur durch eine Leistung, ein Werk, eine Tat, sei es einem erlaubt, sich von einem Vorurteil zu befreien.

Es ist das Gute an Aufzeichnungen, daß sie frei von Berechnung sind. Sie sind zu rasch, sie hatten kaum Zeit, der Kopf, in dem sie entstanden sind, konnte sich noch nicht fragen, wozu sie zu gebrauchen wären.

Leute, die sich einem in einer besonderen Lakaien-Uniform aus Worten nähern. Sie waren zu Diensten und wollen es weiter sein, halten aber nach höheren Herren Ausschau.

Ich habe den Kopf eines Pferdes gesehen, auf einem Bild von Munch, Wildheit und Sklaverei in einem, und weiß nun endlich, warum ich Pferde so *schmerzlich* liebe.

Ich las von den Sprüngen des Gazellenkindes in jener Oase, ein Menschenkind, das vier Meter weit sprang, wie die Gazellen, zu denen es gehörte, und fragte mich, während ich las und frage mich seither: ist es das, was ich mit *Verwandlung* gemeint habe?

Pensées gegen den Tod.
Das einzig Mögliche: sie müssen Fragmente bleiben. Du darfst sie nicht selbst herausgeben. Du darfst sie nicht redigieren. Du darfst sie nicht *einigen*.

The way we become what we constantly name: For years on end Karl Kraus repeated "Swift" to himself, indeed for so long that he actually turned into him in *The Last Days of Mankind*.

People shouldn't simply get rid of prejudices. Only on the strength of an achievement, a deed, or an action should they be permitted to free themselves from a prejudice.

The good thing about notations is that they are free of calculation. They are too swift, they don't have enough time for the head that conceives them to ask how they might be used.

People who approach you with special words resembling a lackey's livery: They have been at your service and wish to remain so, but are already on the lookout for higher patrons.

In a painting by Munch I have seen the head of a horse— wildness and slavery all in one—and now I finally know why I love horses so *painfully*.

I read about the leaps of a gazelle child in that oasis, a human child able to jump four yards like the gazelles to whom it belonged, and while reading I asked and keep asking myself: is this what I meant by *metamorphosis*?

Pensées against death.
The only possibility: These must remain fragments. You must not publish them yourself. You must not edit them. You must not *unify* them.

Alles Schlechte, das du in Gedanken anderen anhängst – woher hast du's?

Wie stolz Menschen sind, wenn man sie an den Charakter erinnert, den sie einmal hatten!

Die Theoretiker ihrer Erfolge sind sterbenslangweilig. Sie müssen beweisen, daß Erfolge stimmen.
Doch nichts stimmt weniger.

Wie erkennt man, daß einer zu Ende gegangen ist? Am Biß? An der Schrift? Am Gelächter?

Der schwerste Verlust des *Usama*, eines arabischen *Ritters der Kreuzzugszeit*: seine Bibliothek von 4000 Büchern.
»Viertausend Bände, wertvolle Schriften! Ihr Verlust wird mir, solange ich lebe, eine Wunde im Herzen bleiben.«

Furcht der Tiere vor dem toten, gehäuteten Löwen:
»Einmal sah ich, wie ein Löwenkopf in eins unserer Häuser gebracht wurde. Als die Katzen ihn sahen, flohen sie aus jenem Haus und stürzten sich vom Dach, ohne je einen Löwen gesehen zu haben. Hatten wir einen Löwen getötet, so häuteten wir ihn ab und warfen den Kadaver von der Festung herab an den Fuß der Bastion. Doch weder die Hunde noch irgendein Vogel näherten sich ihm. Wenn die Raben das Fleisch erblickten, ließen sie sich herab. Doch sobald sie nahe waren, schrien sie und flogen wieder davon!«
Usama, Buch der Belehrung durch Beispiele

All the evil things which, in your thoughts, you pin on others—where did you get them from?

How proud people are when reminded of the character they once possessed.

The theoreticians of their own successes are deathly boring. They need to prove that these successes are deserved. But nothing could be less deserved.

How does one recognize that someone has reached the end? By his bite? By his writing? By his laughter?

The heaviest loss suffered by Usama, an Arab knight from the time of the Crusades: his library of four thousand tomes. "Four thousand folios, precious writings! Their loss will tear my heart for the rest of my life."

The fear of animals confronted by a dead, skinned lion: "I once watched as the head of a lion was brought into one of our houses. When the cats caught sight of it, they fled the house and threw themselves from the roof, even though they never had seen a lion before. Whenever we killed a lion, we skinned it and threw the corpse from the fortress wall to the bottom of the bastion. Yet neither the dogs nor any of the birds approached it. When the ravens caught sight of the carrion, they flew down toward it, but as soon as they were close, they screamed and flew away forthwith."

Usama, The Book of Instruction by Examples

»Beinahe jede Nacht zählt sie jetzt ihre Toten. Sie irrt sich immer. Sie vergißt welche: es gibt welche, die mehr tot sind als die anderen.«   *Jules Renard, Journal*

Es nützt nichts, sich die Wahrheit zu sagen, immerzu die Wahrheit. Die Wahrheit, die sich zu nichts verwandelt, ist Schrecken und Vernichtung.

Der *Ton* der Ägypter ist dein eigener, wie sonst kein Ton. *Tiere* so heilig wie die *Schrift*. Gericht und Waage. Der zerstückelte Tote zu Leben zurückgefügt. Die Totenklage.
Die Totenklage, die dem Toten nichts vorhält.
Zurückfinden zu dem, was der Tote an einem geliebt hat. Das Verhaßte aufgeben, um seinetwillen. Sich für den Toten reinigen. Der Tote als Instanz. Es ist ihm nichts verborgen.
Die Vergangenheit nützen, als Zeit des Toten.

Hoheit der Lobenden. Erst etwas zaghafte Unsicherheit: bist du's? Dann Schulterklopfen, herablassendes Lob, steigender Abschied. Als hätten sie dich vom Boden und damit sich selber aufgehoben.

Sie werfen ihm vor, daß er sein Erinnertes auf die Beine stellt. Es soll doch schwanken, meinen sie, es soll zerfließen, nichts soll man erkennen, alles was bestand, verdiene auseinander gegangen zu sein.

Cervantes und seine *erlebte* Rhetorik. Er selbst ist sein Ritter. Er verhöhnt *sich*.
Seine Hartnäckigkeit: die des Sklaven, der an seiner Befreiung arbeitet.

"She now counts her dead practically every night. She never gets the number right. She forgets some: there are some who are more dead than the others." *Jules Renard*, Journal

It serves no purpose whatsoever to tell oneself the truth and never anything but the truth. The only truth that does not transform itself into nothing is horror and annihilation.

The *tonality* of the Egyptians is your own as no other. *Animals* as sacred as *writing*. Judgment and scales. The dismembered dead reassembled to life. The lament for the dead.
The lament for the dead that does not reproach the dead for anything.
To retrieve what the dead person loved in us. To give up what we hate for his sake. To purify ourselves for the dead.
The dead as highest authority. Nothing is hidden from the dead.
To use the past as the time of the dead.

The loftiness of the eulogists. At first, a certain timid uncertainty: is it you? Then the confirmatory tap on the shoulder, condescending praise, rising farewell. As if they had lifted you, and thereby themselves, from the ground.

They chide him for setting up his memories so sturdily, so upright. They feel that remembrance should sway, that it should flow apart, that nothing should be recognizable; whatever existed before deserves only to disintegrate.

Cervantes and his rhetoric of *experience*. He is his own knight. He mocks *himself*.
His tenacity: that of the slave, working on his liberation.

Das Gleichbleibende, das Unverrückbare der Charaktere: Don Quijote wie Sancho Pansa, und trotzdem, innerhalb strengster Grenzen ihr Reichtum. Wie unscharf, wie unverbindlich, wie weichlich erscheinen, daran gemessen, spätere Romane. Rhetorik im höchsten Maß, aber innerhalb der Charaktergrenzen. Ritter-Rhetorik gegen Sprichwort-Rhetorik. Der Freß- und Friedfertige hat keineswegs immer Unrecht. Die Edel-Reden erregend, weil sie von Freß-Reden abgelöst werden.

Man verzeiht ihm viel, wegen des mystischen Wortes Verwandlung.

Alle Worte, die noch prall von Bedeutung sind – und du verzagst! Genügt es nicht, daß die Worte sich weitergeben?

Eine Aufzeichnung muß wenig genug sein, sonst ist sie keine.

»Diese Energieschübe steigen in Form heißer Plasmaströme aus dem Sonnenkern empor und entfachen dabei (wie sich berechnen läßt) *eine Art Brandungsdonner von unvorstellbarer Lautstärke.*«

Nichts ist mir unerträglicher als die *Mechanik* des Denkens. Darum zerbreche ich seinen Gang nach jedem Satz.

Ungeheurer und gewollter Vorrat: Goethe.
Wo du ihn aufschlägst, bedeutet er dir etwas. Wie ist das möglich? Aber es ist sicher nur möglich, wenn es nicht zu einer Lehre verarbeitet wird.

The constancy, the immutability of the characters: Don Quixote as much as Sancho Panza, and yet, within the most stringent restrictions, their richness. Measured against that, how unfocused, how unengaging, and how flabby later novels appear to us.
Rhetoric at its peak, but within the limits imposed by the characters. The rhetoric of chivalry versus the rhetoric of proverbs.
The conciliatory glutton is by no means always in the wrong. The lofty speeches are exciting because they alternate with speeches of gluttony.

Much is being forgiven to him because of the mystic word "metamorphosis."

All those words still chock-full of meaning—and yet you lose heart! Isn't it enough that the words propagate themselves?

A notation must be sufficiently small—or else it ceases to be one.

"Thrusts of energy rise from the core of the sun in the form of hot plasma streams and, in the process, produce (as can be calculated) *a surf-like thunder of inconceivable volume.*"

Nothing is more unbearable to me than the *mechanics* of thinking. This is why I disrupt its motion after each sentence.

Enormous and deliberate reserve: Goethe.
Wherever you open him, he is full of meaning to you. How is this possible? Surely it is only possible as long as Goethe is not being elaborated into a doctrine.

Das Unerlangbare an Tieren: wie *sie* einen sehen.

Die scheinbare Gerechtigkeit, mit der man das eigene Leben betrachtet.
Zu wirklicher Gerechtigkeit müßte man noch viel älter sein, 300, 500 Jahre.

Hundertjähriger, der den ›Überlebenden‹ aus der Welt schaffen will.

An Jacob Burckhardt ist zu bewundern, daß er nie *über* seine Verhältnisse denkt. Aber was für Verhältnisse das waren!

Erzählen in Katarakten.

Groll macht ihn zutraulicher.

Mächtiger, der vorsichtig von Ohnmacht träumt.

Der Konsequente, der für *jede* Nation ist, auch für solche, die nur zwei Sprecher zählen.

Er geht als Atem in andere ein. Sie lassen ihn gewähren.

Präpositions-Denker.

The unattainable in animals: how they see us.

The seeming righteousness with which we view our life. To achieve genuine righteousness, we would have to be much older, say, by three or five hundred years.

A hundred-year-old who wants to eliminate the "survivor" from the world.

What is admirable in Jacob Burckhardt is the fact that he never thinks about his own circumstances. And *what* circumstances these were!

To tell a story in cataracts.

Rancor makes him more trusting.

A powerful man who cautiously dreams of powerlessness.

The consistent person who speaks out in favor of *all* nations, even those whose language is spoken only by two people.

He enters others as breath. They allow him to have his way.

A thinker of prepositions.

Es ist wahr, daß man sehr viel vergessen hat. Aber was alles nachgewachsen ist und die ›leeren‹ Stellen erfüllt! Das ist das Interessante an einer Lebensgeschichte.

Wieder Pascal.

Der einen nie irritiert hat, nie enttäuscht. Er ist nirgends entliehen. Seine Schlüssigkeit läßt Türen offen. Sogar wenn man mit keinem Wort von ihm einverstanden wäre, möchte man sie wieder und wieder sehen und bedenken. Keine Entdeckung steht ihm im Weg. Glaube und Denken empfindet man bei ihm als einander ebenbürtig.

In den Pensées kommt Pascal zugute, daß er immer *unterbricht*. Von jedem lassen sich die Stücke anders zusammensetzen. Sie bleiben am besten unzusammengesetzt.

Der Ansatz ist sein Eigentliches, und die Reinheit Pascals drückt sich in jedem Ansatz aus.

»Die Vielheit, die sich nicht zur Einheit zusammenschließt, ist Verwirrung, die Einheit, die nicht von der Vielheit abhängig ist, ist Tyrannis.«

Nicht Bilder, nicht Bilder allein. Hie und da ein Bild. Aber du hast die Bilder vernachlässigt. Den Beteuerungen verfallen, hast du dir für die Bilder nicht Zeit genommen.

Sind sie erloschen, eingeschlafen, verfallen?

It is true that I have forgotten a great deal. Yet how much regrowth has there been in the interim and how this growth has filled my "empty" spaces! This is what is interesting about the story of a life.

Once again Pascal:
He never irritates, never disappoints. He isn't borrowed from anywhere. His logical conclusiveness leaves doors open. Even if you do not agree with a single word of his, you want to read his words again and again, so as to think them over. No discovery bars his way. In him you sense the absolute equality of faith and thought.
In the *Pensées* Pascal benefits from the fact that he constantly *interrupts*. In each one, the parts can be assembled differently, but it is best to leave them unassembled.
The beginning is its essential component, and the purity of Pascal is expressed in every one of his beginnings.
"Diversity which fails to merge into unity amounts to confusion; unity independent of diversity amounts to tyranny."

Not images, not images alone. An image here and there. But you have neglected the images. Addicted to affirmations, you failed to take time for images.
Have they become extinguished, did they fall asleep, did they disintegrate?

IX

Er kann sich nach Menschen beinah so sehnen, als ob sie nicht mehr am Leben wären.
Ganz nicht.

Das Schlimme ist nicht, etwas zu *sein*, sondern immer dafür zu gelten.

Wie wunderbar, daß sie alle wieder auferstehen! Aber müssen sie dann gleich gerichtet werden!

Leonardo, der von den Tieren ergriffen war und von der Niedertracht des Menschen, der sie bedrückt.
Sein unablässiges Denken, das ihn nicht schlecht macht.
»Von Eseln, die wir schlagen. O gleichgültige Natur ... und sie verbringen ihr ganzes Leben, indem sie ihren Bedrückern Gutes tun.«
»Von Schafen, Kühen, Ziegen und ähnlichem. Unzähligen von ihnen werden ihre kleinen Kinder weggenommen, und sie werden aufs Barbarischste geviertteilt.«

Es ist die Zeit, in der deine Worte sich überstürzen.
Fall ihnen nicht in die Zügel! Lauf mit!

Der interpretiert den Tod.

IX

He can long for people almost as much as if they were no longer alive.
Though not quite.

The worst is not *being* something but always to be taken for so being.

How marvelous that they will all be resurrected! But do they all have to be judged right away?

Leonardo, who was much affected by animals and by the vileness of humans who oppress them.
His incessant thinking which nevertheless did not pervert him.
"Concerning donkeys, which we beat. Oh, woe for our indifferent nature . . . and yet they spend their entire life doing good to their oppressors."
"Concerning sheep, cows, goats, and innumerable other such animals, whose little ones are taken away from them and then quartered in the most barbarous manner!"

This is the time when our words go galloping away.
No, don't rein them in! Run in stride with them!

That man interprets death.

Es heißt: »Wenn eine Person sich plötzlich ihrer früheren Geburt erinnert und es sagt, bedeutet das sicher den Tod.« Und wenn sie es verschweigt?   *Somadeva*

Aus der Geschichte lernen, daß man nichts aus ihr lernen kann.

Die Kraft des Träumens, meint er, sei an die Vielgestaltigkeit der Tiere gebunden. Mit ihrem Verschwinden sei das Versiegen des Träumens in Sicht.

Daß andere an meinem Leben herumfingern werden, erfüllt mich mit Widerwillen. Unter ihren Händen wird es ein anderes Leben werden. Ich will es aber so haben, wie es wirklich war.
Ein Mittel finden, sein Leben so zu verbergen, daß es nur für die sichtbar wird, die klug genug sind, es nicht zu entstellen.

Gilgamesch ist um nichts weniger zwingend als die Bibel. Er hat *einen* Vorteil über sie: eine feindliche Göttin, gegen die er offen kämpft. Das Weibliche, wie immer angesehen, ist *da*. In der Bibel ist es reduziert da, als Eva.

In einem einzigen Größenwahn, wenn er nur lang genug brach lag, ist Platz für Millionen.

Er sammelte alle Meinungen, um zu zeigen, wie wenige es sind.

It is said: "When a person suddenly remembers his or her earlier incarnation and mentions it, death is sure to follow." And what if that person keeps it secret? *Somadeva*

To learn from history that one cannot learn anything from it.

The power of dreams—so he believes—is tied to the multiformity of animals: with their disappearance one may soon expect the dreams to dry up as well.

That others will fiddle around with my life fills me with dismay. In their hands it will become a different life. Yet I want to keep it the way it really was.
How to find a means of concealing one's life so that it reveals itself only to those intelligent enough not to distort it?

Gilgamesh is in no way less compelling than the Bible. In fact, it has *one* advantage: a hostile goddess against whom the hero openly struggles. The female element, however it may be viewed, is *present*. In the Bible it is there only in a reduced form, as Eve.

Provided it has remained fallow long enough, one single delusion of grandeur may nourish millions.

He collected all opinions to show how few there are.

Sie suchen mich nach ihren Ruinen ab. Ich bin meine eigene.

Mitgefühl ist überwältigend, oder es ist keines. Darum *braucht* man das Wort Erbarmen.

Unergründlich, was aus Autoren in anderen Autoren wird. Es geht nicht nur um Wiederholungen, um pflanzenhaften Schmuck, um Arabesken zu Arabesken, um geliehene Leidenschaft – es geht vor allem um Mißverständnisse, so unauflösliche, daß sie fruchtbar werden. So kommt es zu ganz absonderlichen und rätselhaften Gebilden, zu Autoren, die *größer sind als ihre Vorbilder.*

Es ist nicht die Offenheit allein bei Stendhal, es ist die Offenheit in *jeder* Maskerade.

Wenn es um Tote geht, um das, was ihnen geschieht, bin ich erbarmungslos vor Zorn.
Aber es müssen meine Toten sein. Bei anderen schaue ich mitleidig oder erschrocken zu.

Philosophen, die alles *dazwischen* wissen.

Es könnte sein, daß er sich durch *Kürze* um alles gebracht hat, was an Sätzen lohnt, ihr An- und Abschwellen, Steigen und Fallen, Unglück und Glück. Es könnte sein, daß Sätze nicht gepreßt sein sollten, kein Destillat, sondern eine immerquellende Fülle. Dann hat er sich während aller Jahre des Schreibens um das gebracht, was ihre Lust gewesen wäre und diese Askese der Kargheit vergeblich gepriesen.

They search all over me for their ruins. But I am my own.

Compassion must overwhelm or it is not compassion. Which is why we *need* the word "mercy."

Unfathomable what becomes of authors in other authors. It is not so much a matter of repetition, of flowery ornamentation, of arabesque added to arabesque, of borrowed passion—it is mainly a matter of misunderstandings, so insoluble they ultimately bear fruit. Strange and baffling creatures come into being as a result of this, authors who *are greater than their prototypes.*

It is not the candor of Stendhal alone, it is the candor of *any* masquerade.

When it comes to the dead and what is being done to them, I am merciless in my rage.
But they have to be my very own dead. With others, I merely watch—with fear or with pity.

Philosophers who know everything *in between.*

It is possible that through *brevity* he missed out on everything that is worthwhile in sentences, their swelling and their ebbing, their rise and fall, their misery and their happiness. It could be that sentences should be neither compressed nor distilled, but should pour forth in everlasting fullness. If that should be the case, then in all the years of his writing he has been deprived of its greatest joy, and his preaching the asceticism of frugality has been in vain.

Die schrecklichste Geschichte fand ich heute, in den Erinnerungen einer Frau, der Misia Sert. Ich nenne es die *Fliegenpein* und setze sie wörtlich her:
»Eine meiner kleinen Schlafgefährtinnen war eine Meisterin in der Kunst des Fliegenfangens geworden. Geduldige Studien an diesen Tieren hatten es ihr ermöglicht, genau die Stelle zu finden, durch die man die Nadel stechen mußte, um sie aufzufädeln, ohne daß sie starben. Sie verfertigte sich auf diese Weise Ketten aus lebenden Fliegen und geriet in Entzücken über das himmlische Gefühl, das ihre Haut bei der Berührung der kleinen verzweifelten Füße und zitternden Flügel empfand.«

Von allen Seiten dringt sie ein, die Wehleidigkeit. Sie gilt gar nicht dir selbst. Sie gilt den anderen, die du leben siehst. Du erträgst die Schmerzen nicht, die sie erleiden. Du willst alles von ihnen abwenden, was zu Schmerzen führt. Was ist das? Es ist die Folge dessen, daß du nichts anerkennen kannst, wie es ist. Aber auch nicht, was *war*, was schon vorüber ist, vermagst du anzuerkennen. Alle Geschichte für dich ist falsch. Du liest sie mit zitterndem Herzen. Du willst sie rückgängig machen. Wie macht man Geschichte rückgängig? Durch neue Qualen?

Man soll aus seiner Empfindlichkeit keine Tugend machen. Man mag sie erfahren, und so wie man sie erfahren hat, bewahren. Aber man soll sich mit ihr nicht schmücken. Sie macht den, der sich mit ihrer Ordensreihe brüstet, süchtig. Er braucht mehr und mehr Empfundenes, das er herzeigen kann, und wenn er keines hat, erfindet er's, und es ist danach, erlesen, brüchig, vermodert.

Nebeneinanderlegen darfst du die Sätze schon, sie mögen einander *sehen*, und wenn es sie reizt, dürfen sie einander berühren. Mehr nicht.

Today I found a most horrible story in the memoirs of Misia Sert. I call it *the agony of flies* and quote it here verbatim: "One of my little bed companions has become a real master in the art of catching flies. Patient studies of these insects has enabled her to find the exact spot where one could insert a needle into their bodies to thread them without causing their death. In this way she manufactured strings of living flies and delighted in the heavenly feeling on her skin caused by the desperately scrabbling little feet and the tiny trembling wings."

The woefulness penetrates from all sides. But it doesn't affect you personally. It affects the other people, people you watch while they live. You cannot stand the pains they suffer. You want to avert anything that could cause them suffering. What is this?
It is the result of your inability to acknowledge anything as it actually is. Nor are you able to acknowledge that which *was* and already is past. All of history for you is false. You read it with a trembling heart. You would like to rescind it. But how can one rescind history? Through new sufferings?

People should not make a virtue out of their sensitivity. They may experience it and preserve it as it was experienced. But they should not adorn themselves with it. Sensitivity will make an addict out of anyone who displays its medals on his chest. He will require more and more objects to enable him to demonstrate his sensitivity, and if he runs out of them, he will simply make things up—and his sensitivity will then reveal itself for what it is: precious, brittle, and rotted through and through.

Yes, you may place sentences next to each other, they may *see* each other and, if they should feel that urge, they may even touch each other. But no more.

Wenn er Hölle sagt, ist es, als hätte er seine Strafe darin schon abgebüßt und sei zu jedermanns Zufriedenheit entlassen worden.

Es gibt Diener des Reichtums und Diener des Ruhms. Unschuldig sind beide nicht: sie erwarten Abfälle.

In der Erwartung, mit der dich jeder neue Mensch erfüllt, bist du ein Kind geblieben. In der Enttäuschung danach, sehr rasch ein grimmiger Greis.

Es fehlt ihm die Bewegung von sich weg. Auch wenn er reist – er bleibt immer in eigener Nähe. Er vergißt nie, daß er da ist. Was er sich nimmt, gebührt ihm, denn er hat sich's genommen. Für ihn ist die Welt da, die anderen sind Illustrationen.

Das Wissen, indem es wächst, verändert seine Gestalt. Es gibt keine Gleichmäßigkeit im wirklichen Wissen. Alle eigentlichen Sprünge erfolgen *seitwärts*, Rösselsprünge.
Was geradlinig und voraussehbar weiterwächst, ist bedeutungslos. Entscheidend ist das gekrümmte und besonders das seitliche Wissen.

Dort lesen die Leute zweimal im Jahr die Zeitung, übergeben sich und gesunden.

Dort haben Länder keine Hauptstadt. Die Leute siedeln sich alle an den Grenzen an. Das Land bleibt leer.
Hauptstadt ist die ganze Grenze.

When he says "Hell" it sounds as if he had already served his sentence down there and had been released to everyone's satisfaction.

There are servants of wealth and servants of fame. Neither are innocent: both wait for scraps.

In the expectations you have of any new person you meet, you have remained a child. But in the disappointments that followed, you very quickly became a cantankerous old man.

He lacks the ability to move away from himself. Even when he travels, he always stays close to himself. He never forgets that he is there. Whatever he takes is his due, because he took it. The world is there for his sake; the others are mere illustrations.

In growing, knowledge changes its shape. True knowledge knows no uniformity. All leaps in knowledge occur *sideways*: the way knights move on a chessboard.
Anything that grows in a straight line and in a predictable manner is without significance. It is the skewed and particularly the lateral knowledge that is decisive.

There, people read the newspapers twice a year, then they throw up and recuperate.

There, countries have no capitals. The people all settle at the borders. The country itself remains empty. The whole border is the capital.

Dort träumen die Toten und tönen als Echo.

Dort begrüßen sich Menschen mit einem Schrei der Verzweiflung und verabschieden sich mit Jubel.

Dort stehen die Häuser leer und werden stündlich gefegt: für künftige Generationen.

Dort schließt ein Beleidigter für immer die Augen und öffnet sie heimlich, wenn er allein ist.

Dort beißt man rasch und insgeheim zu und sagt: Ich nicht.

Dort sagt man »du bist« und meint »ich wäre«.

Dort erkennt man Ahnen, für Zeitgenossen ist man blind.

Verweile doch, sagt man und holt den Henker.

Einer, um nicht alt zu sein, *reist* unaufhörlich.
Ein anderer, in derselben Absicht, hält sich vollkommen still.

Im Alter werden die Vorurteile gefährlich. Man ist stolz auf sie. Man ist ihnen dankbar, so als wären sie es, die einem das Leben bewahrt haben. Sie werden auf sonderbarste Weise sehr spät noch aktiv. Man kann sogar von einer Spätblüte der Vorurteile sprechen. Sie werden nicht mehr bekämpft, man setzt

There, it is the dead who dream dreams and resound as an echo.

There, people greet each other with a scream of despair and part from each other in jubilation.

There, the houses are empty and cleaned every hour: for future generations.

There, someone who has been insulted closes his eyes forever, and opens them in secret when he is alone.

There, people bite quickly and furtively, and then say: "It's not me."

There, people say "You are" and mean "I might be."

There, people recognize their forebears, but are blind to their contemporaries.

Stay, someone says, as he goes to fetch the hangman.

One person who *travels* constantly, so as not to grow old. Someone else, with the same intent, who doesn't move a muscle.

In old age, prejudices become dangerous. You are proud of them. You are grateful to them, as if it were they who kept you alive. In the oddest way—very belatedly—they become active, a kind of late blooming of prejudices. You no longer struggle or resist them. You draw them forth separately and

ihnen keinen Widerstand entgegen. Man zieht sie einzeln hervor und besieht sie mit Nachsicht, Produkte einer reichhaltigen Lebenszeit, bewährte Kostbarkeiten, unausschöpfbare Reste. Wenn jemand sie einem vorhält: aber das sind doch Vorurteile! – stimmt man entzückt zu. Wären ihrer nur mehr! Hätte man nicht manche von ihnen auf dem Wege verloren! Der Vorurteilsbesitzer hat sein Gewicht und er fühlt es. Junge, die noch kaum welche haben, sind für ihn Spreu im Wind. Der Vorurteilsbesitzer ist entschlossen, nicht das Geringste von sich, das andere ärgert, aufzugeben.

Alle unvergessenen Gesichter. Seit einigen Jahren kommen keine neuen dazu. Wer jetzt in mein Leben tritt, holt sich aus dem Haufen ein Gesicht. Ich helfe ihm dabei. Er ist nicht er selbst, er ist wie irgendwer aus dem Haufen.

Wie lächerlich, daß man geliebt sein will und *sich kennt*.

Den größten Teil der Zeit verbringen Ameisen *untätig*. Revolution in der Vorstellung von Ameisen.

Kein Traum ist je so unsinnig wie seine Erklärung.

Von der ungeheuren Hinterlassenschaft der Antike sind das Lebendigste die Verwandlungen.
Ihre Wirkungen sind noch immer unerschöpflich. Sie werden nie zu erschöpfen sein.
Wer früh von ihnen erfahren hat, ist – selbst heute – nie verloren. Es ist von den Wundern das Einzige, das glaubwürdig geblieben ist.

examine them tolerantly, they, the products of a rich life, precious valuables you can count on, inexhaustible remains. If someone reproaches you for them, saying: "These are nothing but prejudices!" you assent delightedly. If only there were more of them! If only a few of them hadn't been lost on the way! The owner of prejudices proudly feels his own weight. The young, who hardly have accumulated any prejudices as yet, for him are nothing but straws blowing in the wind. The possessor of prejudices is determined not to give up a single part of himself that might irritate others.

All those unforgotten faces! There hasn't been a new one added now for quite some years. Whoever enters my life now goes and fetches a face from the pile of old ones. I help him find one. He is not himself, he is like someone out of the heap.

How ludicrous that a person wants to be loved, even though he *knows himself.*

Ants spend most of their time being *inactive.* A revolution in our conception of ants?

No dream is ever as absurd as its interpretation.

Out of the enormous legacy left by antiquity, the transformations have retained the most vitality.
Their effects are still inexhaustible. They will never be exhausted.
He who learns of them early is never lost—not even today.
Of all the miracles, this is the only one which has remained credible.

Der *öffnende Wind* Büchners, in jedem Satz. *Diesen* Wind
kenne ich nur von ihm. Es ist kein Atem, es ist Wind, oder
Wind statt Atem. Man denkt nicht an ihn, es weht, es nimmt
einem jede Schwäche und jeden Hochmut.
Ein vergleichbarer Wind ist in der Bibel, aber schwerer, man
kommt nicht ohne Anstrengung wieder weg, man hat Mühe
mit seiner Freiheit. Büchners Wind *ist* Freiheit, zu jedem.

Von den Tieren redet viel, wer sich der Menschen schämt.

Er *sortiert* die Augenblicke, bis sie erlöschen.

S. kommt mit dem Schrecken *zuerst*, er droht gleich mit dem
Furchtbarsten, was er den anderen zudenkt. Hitler hat es an-
fangs verborgen und dann allmählich enthüllt. Die Steigerung
hat er sich immer vorbehalten.
Eine der Hauptwaffen S.'s ist die Achtung des Lebens bei
Amerikanern (und Engländern). Er setzt dagegen die Leicht-
fertigkeit im Umgang mit Menschenleben auf seiner Seite.
53 000 Opfer habe die Rückeroberung von Fao gekostet, viel
mehr als die Amerikaner zehn Jahre Krieg in Vietnam.
Nie ist das Rechnen mit Leichenhaufen so nackt ausgesprochen worden. S. ist ein Assyrer, er hat auch nicht vergessen,
wie die Mongolen Herren von Bagdad wurden. Die Geschichte hört nie auf. Am wirksamsten ist sie in Machthabern, die in
ihr Vorbild und Ansporn finden.

Die Welt ist in rasende Bewegung geraten. Solche Beschleuni-
gungen kennt man von Kriegen und Revolutionen. Jetzt aber
ist es eine Bewegung an sich, *vor* Kriegen oder ohne sie, und
auch die Revolutionen sind vielsinnig geworden.
Es sind Bewegungen der Massen, und zwar in neuer Dyna-

In every sentence, a *wind* that blows things *open*. Only in Büchner. Not a breath, but a wind, or perhaps wind instead of breath. You don't think about it; it just blows, carrying away all our weakness and arrogance.

A comparable wind blows in the Bible, but it is heavier; it cannot be escaped without great effort; the reader must struggle for his freedom. Büchner's wind *is* freedom for everyone.

He who speaks much of animals is ashamed of mankind.

He *sorts* the moments until they become extinguished.

S. immediately comes on with terror, right away he unveils the most horrible threats he intends for the other. Hitler concealed his terror at first and revealed it only gradually. He always kept its intensification to himself.

One of S.'s main weapons is the respect for human life shown by Americans (and Englishmen), which only points up his own side's readiness to sacrifice. The reconquest of Fao alone cost 53,000 victims, much more than the Americans lost during their ten-year war in Vietnam.

Never before have piles of corpses been computed so nakedly. S. is an Assyrian and he has not forgotten how the Mongols became masters of Baghdad. History never ends. It is most forcibly effective in rulers who find in it their models and their incentive.

The world has assumed a frenzied motion. Such accelerations usually signal wars and revolutions. Now, however, it is motion by itself, *preceding* wars or entirely unconnected to them, and revolutions, too, have become ambiguous. They are movements of masses, according to new dynamics,

mik, die niemand noch durchschaut hat; darum schwer verständlich, und mit häufig wechselnden Vorzeichen.

Man ist für sie, weil sie Erstarrungen lösen, es müßte einer schon sehr verdorrt sein, der sie nicht begrüßt. Aber wie sie ausgehen werden, kann niemand sagen. Eines zeigt sich, das unwiderlegbar ist: es gibt keinen voraussehbaren Gang der Geschichte. Sie ist immer offen. In ihrem Sinn handelt niemand, da niemand ihn kennt. Wahrscheinlich ist, daß es ihn nicht gibt. Das würde bedeuten, daß sie in ihrer Offenheit immer beeinflußbar ist, sozusagen in unseren Händen. Vielleicht sind diese Hände zu schwach, um etwas in ihr auszurichten. Aber da wir auch das nicht wissen, sollen wir's versuchen.

Im Geist voller Inhalte haben Vorurteile eine andere Funktion: Dämme des Abwartens.

Nun stehen sie alle zusammen auf, und statt ihn zu beschuldigen, betrachten sie ihn verwundert.

Betrachtet mich, ich bin's. Erkennt mich, daß ich euch erkenne. Sagt mir, wo ihr wart. Habt ihr lange geschlafen. Ich habe euch gehütet, kein Haar ging euch verloren. Ihr seid da. Ihr seid da. Ihr seid da.

Auf verschiedenen Wegen seid ihr gekommen. Ich habe ausgeschaut nach euch, jede Nacht schlief ich ein, um nach euch Ausschau zu halten und hinkte enttäuscht von Nacht zu Nacht.

Ich sehe euch, endlich, und warte auf ein Wort. Es wird das Schönste sein, das schönste Wort aller Sprachen, und da ihr mir's überliefert, entspringt ihm die neue Sprache.

Kann man es Sehnsucht nennen, daß ich so lange gewartet habe. Nein, es ist mehr. Denn dieses Warten hat euch vor jeder Veränderung bewahrt.

which no one has yet been able to fathom, for they are difficult to understand and marked by swiftly changing portents.
We welcome these movements because they loosen what has
become ossified; only someone truly fossilized would refuse
to greet them with some satisfaction. Yet no one can tell
where these movements will lead. Only one thing is incon-
trovertible: the course of history defies prediction. It remains
open at every point. No one acts according to its inner logic,
because no one knows it. Probably this logic doesn't even
exist. If that is the case, then history, in its openness, is
always subject to influence; it is, so to speak, always in our
hands. Perhaps our hands are too weak to accomplish anything. But since we don't even know that for sure, we should
at least try.

In a mind full of contents, prejudices fulfill a different function: barriers for waiting things out.

Now all of them rise together, and instead of blaming him,
they look at him in surprise.
Look at me, it's me. Recognize me, so that I may recognize
you. Tell me where you've been. Did you sleep long? I have
watched over you and you lost not a single hair. You are
here. You are here. You are here.
You have come along different paths. I looked out for you,
each night I fell asleep to keep a lookout for you and, disappointed, I limped from night to night.
Now finally I see you and am waiting for a word. It will
be the most beautiful word, the most beautiful in all languages, and since you are delivering it to me, a new language
will spring from it.
Can this be called longing, my having waited for so long?
No, it is more. For this waiting has protected you from all
change.

Als letztes verlor er die Namen. Ohne daß er's gewahr wurde, lösten sie sich auf in seinem. Er spürte ihre Grenzen nicht mehr, und wenn er sie hörte, wußte er nicht, daß sie's waren. Er merkte nicht mehr, wie sehr sie ihm grollten. Er vergaß, was Ranküne war. Niemand war hungrig. Satte auf allen Straßen. Er lud Passanten zu sich ein, sie zogen es vor, sich zu verirren. Schatten und Personen gingen getrennt.

Er braucht Größere als sich, um mit ihnen zu prahlen.

Als er die letzte Geisel entließ, brach er zusammen und gab den Geist auf. – Weltherrschaft aus Geiseln.

Natürlich ist es richtig, daß ich zu ihnen gehöre, die die Umstrittensten sind. Aber nur aus diesem Grund.
Sonst gehöre ich zu jedem, der ein Gesicht hat.

Er sagt es wieder und wieder, tausendmal sagt er's wieder, wenn dieses Leben *noch beschämender* wäre, er gäbe es nicht auf.
Es ist verwirrend und es bleibt unergründlich.

Wenn diese Intelligenz, die der Mensch nun einmal hat, überhaupt etwas bedeutet, dann sicher, daß sie alles, was sie einsieht, anficht.

Statt der Tiere hält er sich an ihre Formen. Die werden nicht gemordet.

Last of all, he lost the names. Without his being aware of it, they dissolved into his own name. He no longer felt their borders, and when he heard them, he no longer recognized them. He no longer noticed how angry they were with him. He forgot what vindictiveness was. No one was hungry. Well-fed people on all streets. He invited passersby into his house, but they preferred to lose their way. The shadows walked apart from the people.

He needs people greater than himself in order to boast of them.

When he surrendered his last hostage, he broke down and gave up the ghost. — World dominion by means of hostages.

Of course it is true that I belong to the most controversial. But for that reason only.
Otherwise I belong to anyone who has a face.

He repeats it time and time again, he repeats it a thousand times: even if this life were *more shameful* than it already is, he wouldn't give it up.
It is confusing and remains unfathomable.

If there's any purpose at all in this intelligence with which humans have been endowed, then it must be to contest everything it perceives.

Instead of keeping animals, he keeps their shapes. These are impossible to murder.

Welcher Dichter hat nicht zu seiner Fliege gesprochen?
Wen erkenne ich nicht an seiner Fliege?
Wer hält sich nicht eine Fliege, die für ihn trippelt?

Sehr alt blühte er noch auf und erzählte eine Lügengeschichte
nach der anderen. Allen, die ihn hören wollten, rannte er
nach. Man bedrängte ihn bis in den Schlaf, und er sprach immer weiter. Solange er sprach, vermochte er nicht zu sterben.
Er wurde so alt wie der älteste Mensch, sogar älter. Ein wahrer
Strom von Lügen entsprang ihm, fast alle neu, und wer ihn so
sah, verzweifelte nicht und rechnete zuversichtlich mit zwei-,
dreihundert Jahren.

Alles erregt ihn: ein Brief, ein Gespräch. Alles von außen ver-
setzt ihn in Unruhe. Am unruhigsten wird er, wenn man ihn
zum Sprechen verleitet. Dann bricht er los, und er merkt, wie
unverbraucht er voller Kräfte lebt. Das Leben, das er führt, ist
falsch. Er müßte in höchster Aktivität sein und sich die Steigerung erlauben, zu der ihn alles drängt. Aber er sagt nein,
rechts und links nein und ist stolz auf seine Enthaltsamkeit,
und kräht Würde.

Daß man bestehen muß, *obwohl* andere bestehen, die ganz anders sind, daß man es wissen muß und nicht sein darf wie die,
die ganz anders sind, daß man ihnen gerecht werden muß, obwohl sie anders bleiben werden –
wie schwer, wie unsäglich schwer!

Wenn die Neugier nachläßt, liest er wieder einen Griechen.
Da will er alles noch einmal wissen.

What poet has not spoken to his pet fly?
Whom would I not recognize by the fly he keeps?
Who does not keep a fly which scrabbles for him?

He blossomed forth when he was very old and told one lying story after another. He ran after anyone who wanted to listen to him. People pestered him even in his sleep, and he went on talking. For as long as he talked, he was unable to die. He became as old as the oldest person ever, even older. A veritable stream of lies poured forth from him, almost all of them new, and whoever saw him then did not despair, but confidently counted on another two to three hundred years.

Anything excites him: a letter, a conversation. Anything coming from outside makes him restless. He becomes most restive when being lured into talking. Then he breaks free and realizes how full of unspent forces his life is. The life he leads is false. He should be at his peak, allowing himself that intensification to which he is continually prompted. But he says no, he says no left and right, and, crowing with dignity, takes pride in his restraint.

We are obliged to endure *even though* others who are quite different from us endure; we have to realize this and yet are not permitted to be like those others; we must equal them, even though the others will remain different—
how hard, how unspeakably hard!

Whenever his curiosity slackens, he rereads one of the Greeks. Then he wants to know everything all over again.

Vielleicht wußte er nichts. Aber das eine wußte er wohl: was
es bedeutet, nicht mehr da zu sein.

Die Größe Pascals beruht auf seiner Selbstbeschränkung. Nie
hat es eine gegeben, die beredter war. Immer fiel er sich in die
Rede. So liest sie sich, als wäre sie eben erfolgt und eben von
ihm selber unterbrochen worden. Alle kleineren und größe-
ren Sätze, alle Stücke von Sätzen sind wie von heute.

Wäre es ein Gebot der Anständigkeit, das vermeintlich Beste,
das man geschrieben hat, Satz für Satz durchzugehen und zu
widerlegen? Nein, denn man wäre dann einer von den Leuten,
die die eine Hälfte des Lebens rabiat für etwas kämpfen und
die andere Hälfte rabiat für das Gegenteil.
Man soll sich nicht widerlegen. Anstand ist nur: verstummen.

Hast du denn wirklich gedacht, daß ein achtjähriger Krieg
nichts von sich hinterläßt?
S. ist diese Hinterlassenschaft.

Wenn ich noch zu dem komme, was groß war, so groß, daß es
sich aufgespart hat, wenn ich noch erfahren werde, daß es erlaubt ist, es so zu nennen, wird von mir nichts übrig sein und
ich werde wissen, in Ruhe wissen, daß ich dafür gelebt habe,
in seine Nähe zu gelangen.
Dann werde ich mich auch nicht für das Wort ›groß‹ schämen,
denn was unerlaubt daran ist, habe ich zeitlebens bekämpft.

Die Länder mit ihren Sprachfahnen und wie sie losklatschen
aufeinander.

Maybe he knew nothing at all. But one thing he knew very well: what it means not to be around anymore.

The greatness of Pascal lies in his self-restraint. Never has anyone been more eloquent. He constantly interrupts the flow of his writing, so that it reads as if it had been penned this very instant and as if he himself had broken it off. All the shorter and longer sentences, as well as their parts, sound as if they were written this very day.

Would decency dictate that the writer go through what passes for his best writing, sentence by sentence, in order to refute it? No, for then he would be one of those people who spend half of their life fanatically fighting for one thing and the other half of that same life fighting just as fanatically for its opposite.
One should not rebut oneself. The only decent thing to do: to fall silent.

Did you really think that a war lasting eight years would leave no legacy behind?
S. is that legacy.

If I should yet encounter something truly great, so great that it has kept itself in reserve, if, in addition, I should discover that I am permitted to call it that, then there will be nothing left of me, and I shall know, in calm assurance, that I have lived my life just to approach that greatness.
Nor shall I then be ashamed to use the word "great," for I have fought all my life against using it when it was impermissible to do so.

Those countries with their language banners, and how merrily they lay into each other!

Einer, der *noch nie* allein war, trifft auf einen, der immer allein war.

Alle Verlorenen, die Geld haben. Kaufen, kaufen, kaufen, bis sie ersticken.
Alle Glücklichen, die wünschen können, was nicht zu kaufen ist.

Babels Tagebücher, aus dem Jahre 1920. Man erfährt daraus, daß Babel unter den Juden, die er mit Budjonnys Reiterarmee traf, nicht als Jude galt.
Die Tagebücher, aus denen die Erzählungen abgeleitet sind, enthalten viel, es war ein wüstes volles Leben, das er im Krieg unter den Kosaken führte. Die Erzählungen wirken reicher und unmittelbarer. Erinnerung erst gibt Erfahrung ihre eigentliche Unmittelbarkeit.
Babel wurde 1939 verhaftet und schon 1940 in der Lubianka erschossen.
Vor mehr als sechzig Jahren habe ich ihn zuerst gelesen. Sein Ansehen hat sich mir durch nichts, was ich seither gelesen habe, verringert.
Unter allen neueren Russen ist er mir der nächste. Meine Erinnerung an seinen tiefen Respekt vor Gogol und seine Verehrung Maupassants hat mich, wie ich jetzt sehe, nicht getrogen. Über Dostojewski und über Tolstoi hat er kaum zu mir gesprochen.

Das *Gesehene* bei Babel ist seine Welt, wie sie entsteht.
Das *Gehörte* bei ihm sind die Juden. Die Eigenart seiner Erzählungen ist die Art, wie sein Gesehenes sich mit seinem Gehörten durchdringt.
Wie er sich vor Juden versteckt, denen er nicht weniger zugehört als Gorki, einem Russen, und dem Franzosen Maupas-

One who has *never* been alone meets someone who *always* was.

All the lost people who have money: buying, buying, buying, until they suffocate.
All the happy people who are able to wish for that which cannot be bought.

Babel's diaries of the year 1920. We learn from these that Babel was not considered a Jew by those Jews whom he met with Budënny's cavalry.
The diaries from which the tales derived contain a great deal of the wild and rich life Babel led during the war among the Cossacks. Yet the tales seem more colorful and more immediate. Only remembrance endows experience with such immediacy.
Babel was arrested and shot in 1940 in the Lubyanka prison. I read him first more than sixty years ago. His high standing has not been diminished by anything that I have read since then.
Of all the recent Russian writers, he is the one closest to me. As I can see now, my memory of his deep respect for Gogol and of his admiration for Maupassant did not betray me. He hardly spoke to me of Dostoevski or Tolstoi.

With Babel, that which is *seen* is his world as it comes into being.
With him, that which is *heard* is the Jews. The originality of his tales lies in the manner in which what is seen by him mixes with what is heard.
The way he hides from the Jews, to whom he belongs no less than to the Russian Gorki and the Frenchman Maupas-

sant. Immerhin offeriert er jenen eine jüdische Mutter – eine Verbindung, durch die er ihnen ganz unverständlich wird. Etwas Wesensfremderes als Krieg kann es für Babel nicht geben. Eben darum hat er sich dem Kriege auszusetzen. Was den Kosaken bestialische Freude ist, ist ihm nichts als Qual. Aber er muß es genau *sehen*, Qual ist keine Redensart für ihn. Im Tagebuch ist das Sehen noch manchmal zu getreu, in den Erzählungen nie. Babels Verfolgungsgefühl begann früh, durch die Pogrome. Durch die Beteiligung an der Revolution sucht er sich davon zu befreien. Er gerät in den Krieg und dadurch erst recht in die Nähe von Pogromen. Was er in den Erzählungen schreibt, verschafft ihm die Feindschaft führender Kriegsfiguren. Damit beginnt sein Untergang durch die Schergen der Revolution. Vom Erscheinen der ›Reiterarmee‹ an bis zu seinem Ende führt er den Kampf um sein Leben. Er macht sich mit den Trägern der Verfolgung eng vertraut, er verkehrt mit ihrem Oberhaupt. Er weiß, was ihm bevorsteht. Er weiß auch, daß es ihm durch sein Schreiben bevorsteht. Sein Schreiben ist dadurch gelähmt, er versucht es durch ein vorgeschütztes, künstliches Schreiben zu verdecken. Unvorstellbar ist die Angst, in der er gelebt haben muß. Er sieht es alles klar. Noch im Gefängnis bemüht er sich um Manuskripte. Sie sind der Wortlaut der Gefahr. Es ist wahrscheinlich, daß er am Leben geblieben wäre, wenn er nicht geschrieben hätte.

Du hast *nichts* vorausgesehen. Du warst glücklich über die Abwendung der ungeheuren Gefahr, die über der Erde hing. Die Folgen dieser Abwendung hast du nicht zu Ende gedacht, schon um in der Freude zu bleiben. Aber hat irgendwer etwas vorausgesehen? Ist es vielleicht nicht so, daß jede Voraussicht unmöglich geworden ist und wir nur als Blinde planen?

sant. Nevertheless, he offers the Jews a Jewish mother—a connection which made him totally incomprehensible to them.

Nothing was more alien to Babel's nature than war. And that is precisely what prompted him to expose himself to it. What was beastly pleasure to the Cossacks was sheer torment to Babel. But he had to *see* it in all its detail, for to him torment was not an empty phrase.

In the diaries, the seeing is at times too faithful; never so in the tales.

Babel's feeling of persecution started early as a result of the pogroms. He tried to rid himself of this feeling by participating in the revolution. He got involved in the war, which only brought him closer to the pogroms. What he wrote in his tales provoked the enmity of leading figures in the war. This was the beginning of his downfall at the hands of the revolution's henchmen. He fought for his life from the first publication of *Red Cavalry* all the way to his own demise. He fraternized with the thugs who persecuted him and associated with their commanders. He knew what awaited him. And he realized that it would happen because of his writings. His writing became crippled; he tried to disguise his paralysis with pretense and artifice. The fear that must have filled his life is unimaginable. He saw everything with absolute clarity. Even in prison he labored on manuscripts. They are the very words of danger. It is very probable that he would have remained alive if he had not written.

You did not foresee *anything*. You were happy that the immense danger looming over the earth was averted. You did not think through the consequences of this prevention to their ultimate conclusion, if for no other reason than because you wanted to keep your happiness.

But has anyone foreseen anything? Is it not true that all foresight has become impossible and that we make our plans in blindness?

Es ist, als ob nichts mehr verbindlich wäre, was dir durch den Kopf geht. Es geschieht sozusagen nur dir.

Früher war an Gedanken ein offenes Ende da, das ohne Aufhebens nach anderen suchte. Das, könnte man sagen, war die *Hoffnung* des Gedankens. Je entschiedener ich ihn abbrach, umso mehr Hoffnung behielt der Gedanke. Bei jeder Berührung, heimlich, dehnte er sich aus. Es müßte geschildert werden, wie Gedanken *zwischen* Menschen wachsen.

Heute bricht sich der Gedanke vergeblich ab. Die Lust auf andere, auf das Abenteuer in anderen, ist ihm abhanden gekommen. So mag es systematischen Denkern immer zumute sein. Was ich als Lustlosigkeit der Jahre empfinde, gilt ihnen als Legitimation zu ihrem Denken.

Er hat sich mit dem Wort Qual verbündet und sucht es auf Chinesisch.

Die Wortverwüster – was habe ich mit ihnen zu schaffen? Was bleibt von den Mythen unter ihren Messern?

Lob, beleidigend durch das, was es ausläßt.

Tolstois rohe Altersauffassung des Geschlechts: seine Kraft. Er kann gegen sich angehen, ohne zum Schwätzer zu werden.

Ein Mensch, der sich bekämpft, muß etwas zum Bekämpfen haben. Tolstois Bosheit ist seine Gier, für die seine Frau sich an ihm rächt. Beide wollen sich dafür strafen: sie für die Vergewaltigung, der sie nachgab, er für die Gier, die ihn dazu zwang.

Wer sich den Tod nicht ausreden läßt, hat am meisten Religion.

It is as if nothing that passes through your mind is in any way binding. In a manner of speaking, it only happens to you.

There used to be an open end to all thoughts, and each thought blithely set off looking for others. This might be called the *hope* of thought. The more decisively I broke off a thought, the more hopefulness it retained. At each touch, it—but secretly!—expanded. There should be a description of the way thoughts grow *between* people.

But today each thought breaks off in vain. It has lost the desire for others, for the adventure in others. This may be a constant state for systematic thinkers. What to me is the listlessness of old age, to them appears as the legitimation of their thinking.

He has allied himself with the word "anguish" and looks it up in Chinese.

The ravagers of words—what have I got to do with them? What remains of the myths under their knives?

Praise that insults by what it omits.

Tolstoi's crude conception of sex in his old age: his strength. He is able to chide himself without becoming a windbag. A man who struggles against himself needs to have something against which to struggle. Tolstoi's evil trait is his greedy passion, against which his wife takes revenge. Both wish to punish themselves for it: she for the rape to which she yielded, and he for the lust which compelled him to commit it.

He who will not be dissuaded from facing death has the strongest religion.

Zwischen den Tempeln der Jahrtausende der lächerliche Läufer. Alles will er zum Andenken für sich. Das Bild der Pyramide – *sein* Grabmal.

Es bleibt wenig übrig von dem, was man sich jung erträumt. Aber das Gewicht dieses Wenigen!

Diese letzte Konfrontation, das *Ablaufen der Tage* – jetzt sind es nur noch zehn – hat das Glück des vergangenen Jahres zerstört. Ich beginne mich dieses Glückes wie einer kindischen Hoffnung zu schämen.
Der Mond ist für mein Auge in drei Stücke zerbrochen.

Der Tod, als Mittel der Macht, kann nicht *plötzlich* aufhören. Es ist aber ein Prozeß denkbar, der dazu führt. Vor einem Jahr konnte man noch denken, daß dieser Weg beschritten ist. Aber dieses Jahr, dieses herrliche Jahr ist um, und wir sind wieder, wo wir waren.

Alle vergeblichen Gefühle, wie die der Tiere, bevor sie geschlachtet werden.

Der Machthaber verfügt nach Belieben über seine Feinde, mal so, mal so. Vielleicht bleibt es endlich dabei, daß S. gehen muß. Was nimmt er mit? Wo verbringt er den Rest seiner Tage? Man sieht ihn vor sich als Hundertjährigen, wie er Knaben über den Kopf fährt.
Sein vorbildliches Familienleben. Der Mann, der Millionen Tote aushält, weil er auf Vergasungen gebaut hat.

Dieser Wunsch zu bleiben, eine Art von Buchhaltung.

Between the temples of the millennia, the ludicrous runner. He wants everything as a souvenir for himself. The picture of the Pyramids—his funeral monument.

Little remains of youth's dreams. But how great is the weight of that little!

This last confrontation, the *passing of days*—now there are only ten left—has destroyed the happiness of this past year. I'm beginning to be ashamed of this happiness as of a childish hope.
In my eyes, the moon has broken up in three pieces.

Death, as a means of power, cannot stop *all of a sudden*. But it is possible to imagine a process that may lead to that. A year ago, I still could believe that this path was being followed. But that year, that wonderful year, is now a thing of the past and we are back where we were before.

All those futile feelings, like those of animals about to be slaughtered.

The ruler deals with his enemies as he sees fit, one time this way, one time that way. Perhaps it finally will be decided that S. has to go. What will he take with him? Where will he spend the rest of his days? We can imagine him, a hundred years old, gently passing his hand over the brows of young boys.
His exemplary family life. The man who can bear millions of dead, because he put his faith in extermination by gas.

This desire to stay, a kind of bookkeeping.

Wäre es richtiger, wenn nichts von einem Leben bliebe, gar nichts? Wenn der Tod bedeuten würde, daß man in allen, die ein Bild von einem haben, auf der Stelle erlischt? Wäre es vornehmer gegen die Kommenden? Denn vielleicht ist alles, was von uns bleibt, ein Anspruch an sie, der sie belastet. Vielleicht ist der Mensch darum nicht frei, weil zu viel von den Toten in ihm bleibt und dieses Viele sich weigert, je zu erlöschen.

Der Durst des Vergessens – unstillbar?

Es gibt manche Tote, nach denen man sich *nie* sehnt. Sehr kostbare sind darunter.

Zaumzeug des Witzes. – Er redet Leuten solange zu, bis sie ihn übervorteilen. Dann kann er sie verachten.

Er hat mehr Würde, als er erträgt. Wenn er sie ablegt, kriecht er.

Er will gesucht sein, um sich besser zu verbergen.

Seine wildeste Passion: die Dankbarkeit. Es ist zu verwundern, daß er daran nicht wie an einer Spiel-Leidenschaft in Stücke gegangen ist.

Er vergrößert neue Berühmtheiten durch alte. Er anerkennt alte Berühmtheiten durch neue. Sein Wechselgeschäft.

Would it be better if nothing remained of our lives, nothing at all? If death meant our instant obliteration in the minds of all who have had images of us? Would this be more considerate of those who follow? For it may well be that what remains of us constitutes a claim on them, a burden they are forced to carry. Perhaps human beings are not free because they contain too much of the dead and because this surplus refuses ever to be abolished.

The thirst for forgetting—unquenchable?

There are some who are dead and for whom one *never* longs. Including some very dear ones.

Wit as bridle. He goads people for so long until they get the better of him. Then he can despise them.

He has more dignity than he can bear. When he takes it off, he crawls.

He wants to be sought, so as to better conceal himself.

His wildest passion: gratitude. It is amazing that it didn't lead to his breakdown, as a passion for gambling might have done.

He uses old celebrities to make new ones grander. He uses new celebrities to confer recognition on the old ones. He's in the exchange business.

Einer kennt kein Bild. Er hat ohne Bild gelebt. Er hat nie gewußt, daß es Bilder gibt.
Das erste Bild.

Im Mythos finde ich mich zuerst. Solange es mir natürlich ein-
geht wie Atem, nenn' ich's Mythos. In Zeiten, da es sich ver-
schließt, heiß' ich es anders. Ich lege es dann beiseite und
erwarte die Wiederkehr seiner Einfalt. Verwirrung ist der
Mythos nie, selbst das Entsetzlichste – als Mythos hat es Rich-
tung und Kraft und schließlich Sinn, er darf nur nicht in die
Augen springen.

Zu einer *anderen* Vergangenheit finden, mit Menschen, auf
die du dich noch nie besonnen hast.
Die Vergangenheit jener drei Bücher lähmt dich. Sie ist *zu sehr
wahr*.

Wie haben sie mich aufgeregt, die noblen Lebensverlasser, wie
habe ich mich gemüht, ihnen zu trotzen und abzusprechen,
was sie sehr wohl erfahren haben.
Jetzt denke ich mit Zärtlichkeit an sie, sie könnten noch da
sein – würde ich ihnen jetzt zureden?
Einer soll mir zurückkommen, *ein Einziger*, und ich geb's auf.
Solange aber keiner zurückkommt, *bleib* ich.

Aus der Bibel kamen sie auf ihn zugerannt.

Das eigentliche geistige Leben besteht im *Wieder-Lesen*.

Aus sehr vielen Schicksalen, von denen man erfährt, bildet
sich ein eigenes versäumtes Schicksal.

A certain person doesn't know a single picture. He has lived without pictures. He never knew that pictures existed. His first picture.

I find myself first in myth. If something enters me as naturally as breath, I call it myth. If it closes itself off to me, I call it something else. I then put it aside and await the return of its simplicity. Myth is never confusion, even at its most horrifying; myth has direction and strength and, ultimately, meaning—just as long as it isn't too obvious.

To find a *different* past, with people in it you have never thought of before.
The past of these three books paralyzes you. It is *all too true*.

How much they have upset me, those noble leave-takers from life: how much have I tried to defy them, and to dispute what they have experienced personally.
Now I think of them with tenderness. If they were still here—would I still try to persuade them?
Let just a single one come back, *just a single one*, and I'll give it up.
But as long as none does, I *remain*.

They came running to him straight out of the Bible.

True spiritual life consists in *rereading*.

The great many fates we learn about combine to form a single lost destiny.

Viel Zeit hat man daran gewandt, dem Leben sozusagen unter die Arme zu greifen. Es war vielleicht verlorene Zeit. Aber es will nicht anders gewesen sein. Leichtigkeit, gewiß, ist Glück. Ich beuge mich vor der Schwere.

Er besteht nur noch aus den wenigen Worten, die er zu oft wiederholt hat.

Beschränkung auf das, was einen wirklich etwas angeht? Eben das macht das Elend und die Glorie des Menschen aus, daß er nach dem fragen muß, was ihn nichts angeht.

Wenn er sagt, er glaubt an nichts als Verwandlung, so heißt das, er übt sich im Entschlüpfen, wohl wissend, daß er dem Tod noch nicht entschlüpfen wird, aber andere, einmal andere.

I have spent much time lending life a helping hand, so to speak. And this may well have been time lost. But it refuses to have been otherwise. Lightness undoubtedly is happiness. But I bow to heaviness.

By now he consists only of those few words he has repeated too often.

Restriction to merely that which concerns us as individuals? It is precisely both our misery and our glory that we are compelled to query that which does not concern us.

When he says that he does not believe in anything but transformation, this means that he practices a kind of slipping away, fully aware that he himself will not succeed in eluding death—but others, someday others.